EGMONT PRESS: ETHICAL PUBLISHING

Egmont Press is about turning writers into successful authors and children into passionate readers – producing books that enrich and entertain. As a responsible children's publisher, we go even further, considering the world in which our consumers are growing up.

Safety First
Naturally, all of our books meet legal safety requirements. But we go further than this; every book with play value is tested to the highest standards – if it fails, it's back to the drawing-board.

Made Fairly
We are working to ensure that the workers involved in our supply chain – the people that make our books – are treated with fairness and respect.

Responsible Forestry
We are committed to ensuring all our papers come from environmentally and socially responsible forest sources.

For more information, please visit our website at
www.egmont.co.uk/ethicalpublishing

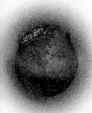

DAVID DONOHUE

MOON MAN

EGMONT

Also by David Donohue

Walter Speazlebud

David Donohue spent a lot of his childhood standing in the school corridor for spelling backwards when he should have been spelling forwards, and for being a 'cheeky little pup'. As well as writing for children, David is a songwriter and a music consultant for film, but he's first and foremost a backwards speller. And when he is stopped in the street by people asking him to spell backwards, he always replies 'b-a-c-k-w-a-r-d-s', because he's still a cheeky pup.

Play the Moon Man game and hcum, hcum erom at www.moonmanonline.com

for Herbie and Jacquie

EGMONT

We bring stories to life

First published in Great Britain 2006
by Egmont UK Ltd
239 Kensington High Street, London W8 6SA

Text copyright © David Donohue 2006
Cover illustration copyright © John Fordham 2006

The moral rights of the author and illustrator have been asserted

All photographs courtesy of NASA. www.nasa.gov

ISBN 978 1 4052 1998 3
ISBN 1 4052 1998 X

3 5 7 9 10 8 6 4

A CIP catalogue record for this title is available from the British Library

Offset by Avon DataSet Ltd, Bidford on Avon, Warwickshire
Printed and bound in Great Britain by the CPI Group

Stnetnoc

	Drowerof	1
	Eugolorp	5
1.	Na Lausunu Yob	7
2.	A Ylpeed Gnipeels Dadnarg	14
3.	Eno Gel Retrohs Naht Eht Rehto	26
4.	Eno Tnaig Pets	34
5.	A Yzarc Elat	43
6.	On Dadnarg	50
7.	Na Noitativni Ot Levart	56
8.	A Ykaerf Kcirt	65
9.	A Wef Ssorc Sdrow	73
10.	Eht Elibomooz Stih Eht Daor	79
11.	Eht Gib Noisiced	91
12.	A Oreh On Erom	100
13.	Eht Tsim Latrop	106
14.	A Esirprus Ni Emit	114
15.	'Nikibrotom	130
16.	Eht Yknow Tekcor	135
17.	A Elbirret Noitasilaer	143
18.	A Dam Aedi	146
19.	Gnivid Rof Seulc	152
20.	Srekcus Dna Srekcuz	159
21.	Bob Seog Dam	164
22.	Eht Elbaveilebnu Hturt	170
23.	A Yrev Ssorc Noitanimaxe	181

24. Eno Tsal Ecnahc 188
25. Ranul Enutpen Snruter 195
26. A S'yad Gniniart 203
27. Eybdoog Teews Dlrow 207
28. Og Ollopa Og 222
29. Cinap Kcatta 224
30. Eht Elgae Sah Dednal 231
31. Ecafrus Noisnet 235
32. A Gib Pets Rof A Llams Nam 242
33. Yrrah Steg Hcir 253
34. Eht Oreh Snruter 260
35. Eht Hturt Ta Tsal 263
36. Lla Steb Era Ffo 269
37. Spetstoof No Eht Noom 272
Eugolipe 276
Stnemegdelwonkca 278

Drowerof

Imagination is more important than knowledge.
Knowledge is limited. Imagination encircles
the world.

Albert Einstein

Type the words 'moon landing 1969' into an internet search engine and, chances are, you will find many theories on how it never actually happened, how it was faked. Now, most people think that it doesn't matter what the non-believers say, because the moon landing in 1969 is now accepted as one of the greatest achievements of Man and no two-bit doubting Thomas is going to take that away from us. And I agree. Those words 'This is one small step for Man, one giant leap for mankind' now resonate in our minds, as if they had been spoken by God.

I should tell you that the story you are about to read is almost as crazy as any other story claiming the moon landing was faked. It is definitely *as crazy as the notion that the moon landing actually did happen.* Consider this: seventeen years after Apollo 11 went to the moon, the Space Shuttle Challenger exploded 73 seconds into its flight due to the failure of a seal in the rocket booster. If NASA failed to take a shuttle into space in 1986, could they have successfully launched a rocket in 1969 and landed two men on the moon and taken them home safely?

Fake or real, this is what the Apollo mission stands for: the power of the imagination (or **Noitanigami** as you'll call it after reading this book): the single most important element in a project as ambitious as landing a man on the moon. It was the imaginations of the rocket scientist Werner Van Braun and NASA's engineers that took the Apollo rocket into space and beyond that, into history. However, though their imaginations had no bounds, their skills as engineers most definitely did; while sending a rocket into space was relatively easy, landing on the moon and guaranteeing the astronauts' safe return was not as simple.

This is the first time my version of events has been told. You might well find it more crazy than NASA's version, but I don't believe you can argue with this: those who are chosen to be history-makers are often the most unlikely sorts, plucked from a hum-drum world to dance to a magical tune whose composer is unseen.

Let me tell you a story about a curly-haired boy with a peculiar approach to spelling words and an imagination as big as the moon itself. This story may seem stranger than fiction but it may also be truer than the 'truth'. You decide!

Eugolorp

Walter leaned up against a white wooden fence in the glare of the morning sunshine. He felt as if he had just woken up from a nap. A slight dizziness made him reach out and hold on to the fence to steady himself. He took a deep breath. Wherever he was, it was summer – giant palm trees swayed in the breeze against a hazy-blue sky. Cars drove by, looking as if they had just jumped out of the pages of his dad's *Vintage Classics* magazine; a red Corvette, a yellow Dodge Charger, a blue Pontiac, a long black Chevrolet. A bunch of teenagers strolled by, looking sleepy and happy and wearing old clothes and shoes like those in the window of the Nittiburg charity shop.

Walter glanced down to check what *he* was wearing. Phew! He still had on his blue T-shirt, grey corduroys and black and red stripy trainers. At least he didn't have a flowery shirt with a pointed collar, like some of those teenagers were wearing!

Nearby, a radio played a song with a fast thumping beat and a lot of 'Sha, la, la's'. Miss O'Connor had once told the class that they had used 'Du-waps' in the fifties, 'Sha la la's' in the sixties, and that the seventies were all about 'Hey, hey, hey'.

Walter could scarcely believe it – it had actually worked – he was now back in the sixties! Good ol' Grandad!

Na Lausunu Yob

Walter Speazlebud was an ordinary boy and, like all ordinary boys, there were certain things about him that were extraordinary or, at the very least, un-ordinary. First, Walter could spell and pronounce any word or name backwards, and this unusual talent made him a regular guest on national TV, where he was known as **Retlaw Dubelzaeps**. Secondly, he was fascinated by the worlds of astronomy and space travel, particularly the Apollo 11 moon landing of 1969. However, apart from Walter's beloved grandad, his teacher, and his parents, few people paid much attention to this – they were much more interested in his backwards spelling talents – but to Walter, astronomy and space travel were the most important things in his life. They were the passions around which he wove his dreams.

Walter's bedroom, a small upstairs room in a

modest, pebble-dashed house on the edge of an ordinary village called Nittiburg, looked more like the attic of an astronomy professor than the bedroom of a ten-year-old boy: photographs of Mars, Jupiter, Saturn, Uranus, Neptune, Pluto and Venus covered one entire wall, while the opposite wall was covered in bookshelves, heaving with dog-eared encyclopedias and books on space travel and astronomy. By his bed sat an antique telescope on a rickety tripod and, above the bed, Walter's greatest hero, the astronaut Neil Armstrong, smiled down on him, his fellow astronauts Buzz Aldrin and Michael Collins on either side. Alongside was another photograph of Neil Armstrong, with his arm around Walter's other hero, his granduncle Bob Speazlebud, who had once been an aeronautical engineer for NASA.

Tinted by the fluorescent green glow of the plastic stars scattered across the ceiling, Walter lay in his bed listening to his mum, Peggy, read to him. Reading was difficult for Walter, at least reading forwards, and, ever since he was a baby,

Peggy read to him every night. Walter *could* read forwards, but only if he pored over every word, reversed it, then flipped it back again in his mind; so it was much easier to lie there and let Peggy's gentle voice take him to the moon and beyond, to the stars, and deeper still into the mysteries and the magic of outer space.

Tonight, however, Walter seemed distracted, nervous, lost in his thoughts. Peggy stopped reading, placed *The Complete History Of Outer Space* on the bedside table, then leaned over and kissed Walter, her only child, on the forehead.

'I know you're worrying about your grandad,' she whispered.

Walter nodded, his eyes as moist as dawn grass.

'You know he loves you more than anybody in the world?'

'More than he loves Mrs Frost's Xtra Strong Mints?'

'Well, maybe not quite that much,' said Peggy with a laugh.

'As much as I love the moon.'

'Exactly,' said Peggy. 'As much as you love the moon.'

'***Doog Thgin***,' said Walter.

'***Doog Thgin***,' replied Peggy.

As his mother left the room Walter switched off the bedside light and looked through the window at the night sky. The moon, almost full, was creeping into the window frame like an old friend coming to say good night.

'Luminous glass ball floating in a pool of stars,' Walter whispered to himself over and over, like a mantra to help him to relax.

Now, you might say that the moon looked like no such thing – it simply looked like a full moon in a starry sky – and it would be hard to disagree, but it was Walter's imagination, more than anything else, which defined his place in the world and, indeed, sometimes made his life difficult.

'I'll walk on the moon one day,' Walter had once told a particularly nasty old teacher, who promptly ordered him to stand in the hallway for being 'childish and ridiculous'.

From that moment onwards Walter shared his dreams with nobody except Grandad.

Walter sat up, reached over and brought the eyepiece of his telescope to his left eye. He pointed the fat end through the window and adjusted the focus until the moon was so close that he could clearly imagine walking upon its sandy surface, one giant step after another.

'This is one big step for a small man,' he said aloud, with a chuckle, reciting the words his grandad had jokingly suggested he should say when he finally fulfilled his greatest dream.

Walter heard the sound of singing coming from the room next door. It was the unmistakable, if unmusical, voice of his beloved grandad.

'Ho Ynnad Yob,
Eht sepip eht sepip era gnillac,
Morf nelg ot nelg
Dna nwod eht niatnuom edis . . .'

The song brought a smile to Walter's face. It was

'Danny Boy', *backwards*. Grandad Speazlebud was the only other person Walter knew who could spell, speak or, for that matter, sing backwards. Of course, Walter's parents and some of the towns-folk had taught themselves certain backwards words and phrases, but nobody came close to Grandad.

Suddenly the singing stopped, as if the old man had forgotten the words.

Walter fell back on to his bed with a sigh, his curls spreading against the pillow. If you were to have taken a close look at Walter's face at that moment you may have noticed the glinting track mark of a single tear which had made its way from his big green eyes down his freckly cheek.

Walter opened his eyes and began to sing, quietly at first, then louder and louder. '***Ho Ynnad Yob, eht sepip eht sepip era gnillac . . .***'

He heard his grandad's voice again, now singing along with all his might. It brought a smile to Walter's face and made his eyes glow bright like

the plastic stars on the ceiling, like that luminous
glass ball floating above him in its pool of stars.

A Ylpeed Gnipeels Dadnarg

The following morning Walter entered his grandad's room and found the old man sleeping deeply. *'Doog Gninrom,'* he whispered as he sat down.

As he waited for him to wake up, Walter noticed how the old man's bushy eyebrows and thinning hair were almost as white as the pillow on which he slept. He noticed, too, how his frail body barely made a bump beneath the blankets these days, and how the skin on his hands was so thin that he could see wiry purple veins running in all directions, like the plumbing beneath the kitchen sink. Then he looked at the photograph above the bed. It showed Grandad with his arm around his younger brother, Bob. He thought about how Bob's passion for space and aeronautics had taken him to America to fulfil his dreams.

But if Bob Speazlebud was a hero to Walter, he was also a mystery: in the many, many years since the moon landing Bob had never spoken about it to anybody; in fact he hardly spoke at all – he had become withdrawn, angry, and not very likeable. Indeed, Walter avoided visiting his granduncle as much as he could, and he was quite happy about the fact that he had managed to steer clear of him for almost a full year.

'I wonder what happened to him,' Walter said, repeating a question that he had often asked but to which nobody could ever give him a satisfactory reply.

Grandad made a deep breathing sound like a sigh. Walter reached out and placed his hand gently on his shoulder. Recently, Walter had realised that there was something not quite right with Grandad. Once, when they returned from a walk together, Grandad couldn't remember where they had been, or the people whom they had met on their way. And then there was the day that Grandad wandered off and was discovered hours later, down by the river, lost and confused.

'Your grandad needs a lot of care now, maybe more than we can give him,' Peggy had said recently.

'There's nothing wrong with Grandad,' Walter had protested, although he knew in his heart that it wasn't true.

Then Walter had gone outside and chased Maharaja the cat around the garden like a demented demon, and he had gone to bed without saying good night, because he knew that what his mother really meant was that Grandad Speazlebud would soon be going 'up the hill', to the Nittiburg Nursing Home, where all the old people go, sooner or later.

Walter's eyes drifted to the bedside table where he noticed a red gemstone, the size of a small acorn, half-hidden amongst the bottles of tablets and medicines. He hadn't seen it before and, being curious, he took the stone and twirled it between his thumb and forefingers. It felt warm and, strangely, seemed to get warmer the longer he held it. Was he dreaming, or was the stone now tingling his skin as if charged by a low-voltage current? He smiled to himself. What if it's some kind of wishing stone? *If it is*, he said to himself, *I'd send Grandad back in time to when he was young and healthy again, when we went fishing together, back to when he was a carpenter and woodcarver, back to the time when he travelled around the world.*

And that made him think of some of Grandad's crazy travel stories, made even more wonderful to Walter by the fact that they supposedly happened in another time: Grandad's trip to Egypt had, according to him, coincided with the building of the pyramids; his visits to Italy had, once, involved watching Michelangelo paint the ceiling of the Sistine Chapel; another had him engaging in an evening of stargazing with Galileo Galilei; and during his visit to Machu Picchu in Peru, Grandad claimed, he had helped the Incas to create a device to bring heavy stones up the steep Andean mountains!

There was another story that Walter never tired of hearing. It was about a deer and, as he closed his eyes, with the warmth of the gemstone keeping him cosy, he imagined he could hear Grandad's gentle voice, as if he was awake and telling the story himself:

'One day I was walking home through the woods when I saw a deer crossing the road. Suddenly a truck came around the bend. The driver was going too fast to stop so I shouted at the deer but, in a state of panic, I said the word "deer" backwards, "***Reed!***" He didn't move, so I shouted it again and again. On the third "***Reed***", the deer zipped backwards and across the road, escaping the truck by inches.'

'Is that true?' Walter would always ask.

'Of course,' Grandad would always reply. 'And that's when I discovered the power of ***Noitanigami***.'

Walter liked that word. It was 'imagination' backwards and, even though he could never explain why, it always made him feel good, like the words 'pebble', 'sooth' and 'scrumptious', or the backwards words *noitartnecnoc*, *elcycib* and *rotagilla*.

When, after a while, Grandad had still not woken up, Walter placed the stone back on the bedside table, then he leaned over and whispered in his ear, 'Miss O'Connor is showing a documentary on the moon landing this morning. I'll tell you all about it when I get back.'

Now, if you had been observing Grandad Speazlebud's features at the moment Walter turned that door handle and slipped quietly from the room, you might have noticed the edges of his mouth tighten ever so slightly to form what could, with just a little imagination, be interpreted as a smile.

When Walter arrived downstairs his dad, Harry, was standing by the window, concentrating deeply as he changed the settings on the Friendly Fly-catcher.

Walter gently lifted Maharaja off a chair, gave him a peck on the nose and placed him on the floor. Then he sat down at the table.

'*Doog 'ninrom, Dad.*'

'*Doog 'ninrom, Retlaw,*' replied Harry as he made some final adjustments. The Friendly Flycatcher was a trapping device designed to catch flies in a small cage and transport them, via a mini cable-car, across the room and out through the window, where it released them, unharmed, back to nature. Harry was an inventor – albeit a spectacularly unsuccessful one – and his boyish face, sparkly eyes and scraggly auburn hair lent him the appearance of an overgrown elf permanently up to devilment.

'When can we test-run the Zoomobile?' asked Walter.

This was Harry's newest invention: a four-seater, glass-covered, animal-proof automobile that was designed to allow its passengers to drive up close to wild animals in the zoo.

'Any day now, son, just as soon as I fit it with the Speazlebud Synchronised Suspension System.'

'Remember our test-run in the Loomobile,

Dad? You almost got sucked down the toilet.'

'Ah yes, but it didn't have the Speazlebud Synchronised Suspension System like the Zoomobile will have,' said Harry, sitting down beside Walter. 'And who invented speed bumps anyway?'

Walter smiled. He loved his crazy dad.

Peggy came through the back door, her dungarees spattered with flecks of luminous paint and her hair tied haphazardly with a ribbon. Her day-glo paintings brought in enough money to support a modest lifestyle for the Speazlebuds, but little more.

'*Doog gninrom*,' she said, giving Walter a kiss on the cheek.

'*Doog gninrom*,' he replied.

'Before I forget,' said Peggy, '*The Friday Night Late Show* just called. They have a cancellation for tomorrow night.'

'The only time they ever call me is when somebody cancels,' said Walter sulkily.

'It's extra pocket-money, Walt,' said Harry.

Walter shrugged his shoulders. 'I suppose,

but I'm getting tired of spelling backwards on TV. It seems . . . pointless.'

The sound of Grandad coughing could be heard coming from upstairs.

'He must have just woken up,' said Walter. 'He was asleep when I went in.'

'I'll take him up some breakfast in a while,' said Peggy as she joined them at the table.

'Miss O'Connor is showing a documentary on the moon landing today,' said Walter.

'Will Annie Zuckers be there?' said Peggy.

'She's in my class,' said Walter with a quizzical look, 'so I suppose she will. Why?'

'Oh, no reason, just that Grandad says you like her.'

Walter dug his spoon deep into his chocco-pops. 'How come Grandad can barely remember his own name, yet he can remember me saying something that even *I* can't remember saying?'

'I'm sorry. I shouldn't . . .'

'Aah, 1969. The moon landing,' said Harry, trying to bring the conversation back to the subject

Walter loved to discuss. 'I was only a boy, but I remember it well. Your grandad let me stay up late to watch it.'

But Walter had something more important to talk about. 'Does Grandad *have* to go into a home?' he asked. 'Why can't he stay here, where he belongs?'

Peggy put her hand on Walter's shoulder. 'It's becoming harder to give him the care and attention he needs, Walter. He could wander off again.'

'But most of the time he's fine,' protested Walter. 'It's just that, sometimes, he forgets and gets mixed up. That's all.'

'I know it's hard, Walter,' said Harry, 'but we have put him on the waiting list for a bed. It could be months, it could be weeks . . . or it could be sooner.'

'Maybe if Bob would come to visit him it might help,' said Walter. 'He talks about him all the time. He says that when Bob was my age he looked at the moon every night, too, and he had more books about space than I have.'

'Walter,' said Harry, 'you know that Bob hasn't visited Grandad since he came back from America a long, long time ago. He's a deeply unhappy man and nobody knows why.'

'Was Uncle Bob *really* an engineer for NASA?' said Walter.

'Apparently,' said Harry. 'Didn't he give you all those books on aeronautics and the telescope you have beside your bed?'

'We don't know for sure if they were from him,' said Walter. 'They arrived with no letter and no return address.'

'That's Granduncle Bob for you,' said Peggy, 'He's odd, and he's not going to change now!'

'Grandad has a saying,' said Walter. '"It's never too late to be what you might have been."'

'And what do you think *might* Bob have been?' said Peggy.

'Happy.'

'Maybe,' said Peggy.

The doorbell rang.

'That'll be Levon,' said Walter as he hopped from his chair, grabbed his bag and ran towards the door.

Eno Gel Retrohs Naht Eht Rehto

Nittiburg was a quaint but unremarkable village, just an hour from the city. The railway track, which ran along Station Road, defined the boundary of the village on one side while, across the village, a natural forest of pine and spruce surrounded the school and ran up the steep Nittiburg Hills, around the nursing home and the stately Georgian mansions that overlooked the town.

Walter and his best friend Levon made an odd-looking pair as they walked through those winding streets on their way to school. Levon Allen was tall and gangly with short, spiky hair, and a pronounced limp, while Walter, though not small, barely reached Levon's shoulder, and his wild curly hair covered his ears.

The boys turned on to Main Street, past the old church on the corner, its granite spire piercing the clouds. Mrs Green, the grocer, was busy arranging her prize-winning vegetable display.

'I bet Mrs Green will speak backwards to her favourite boy,' said Levon, who loved placing bets as much as Walter loved staring at the moon.

'I bet she won't,' replied Walter. 'She's too busy trying to balance that carrot on top of her carrot pyramid.'

'Whatcha bet?' said Levon.

'Five dried apricots, slightly squished,' said Walter.

'Betcha half a chocolate bar nibbled by a Dachshund,' said Levon.

'You're on.'

'*Ylevol yad, Retlaw*,' said Mrs Green as the boys walked by.

'*Ylevol yad*,' replied Walter unenthusiastically.

'Told you so,' said Levon.

'*Sti na yletulosba lufrednow yad deedni*,' Mrs Green continued, proudly speaking the language of the most famous boy in Nittiburg.

'That's scary,' said Walter, when they had

passed by. 'She'd be better off learning Spanish or French or something useful.'

'My dad says that the perfect woman is a woman who knows ten languages and can't say "no" in any of them,' said Levon.

'I don't get it.'

'Neither do I.'

A car slowed down and the passenger window rolled down. A young boy stuck his head out. 'Crocodile,' he shouted.

'E-l-i-d-o-c-o-r-c,' said Walter.

'Pronounce it,' said the boy, rudely.

'*Elidocorc*.'

'You're right, **Retlaw Dubelzaeps**,' said the boy with a scowl, as he checked the piece of paper on which the word was written. 'Now ask me one.'

'Mum,' said Walter.

The boy thought about it for a moment. 'M . . . u . . . m.'

'Genius,' said Walter.

'I want a backwards-speller certificate with your autograph on it, or else I won't watch you on

TV ever again,' said the boy, while his father impatiently revved the car.

Walter took a **_Dubelzaeps_** Spelling Certificate from his bag, signed it and handed it to the boy. The boy's head popped back into the car like a snail into a shell as the car revved up, then sped away with a beep of the horn.

'Nice kid!' said Levon.

'Some people think I'm a freak, ready to entertain them whenever they feel like it,' said Walter.

'I don't know about *some* people,' said Levon, 'but that's definitely how I feel.'

Walter pretended to throw his squished-up apricots at his friend.

'Hey, they're my apricots,' said Levon. 'You lost the bet.'

Walter handed over his apricots.

'I have a special bet for you today,' said Levon, as the boys continued down the hill.

'What's that?'

'I bet the world is gonna end in the year 2095. I bet a hundred marbles and a half-chewed

Harry Potter and the Philosopher's Stone.'

'Chewed by you?'

'No, stoopid, my black rabbit.'

'And I bet you my fishing rod that within the next one hundred and fifty years man will be able to *think* himself into space,' said Walter.

'I bet you're right,' said Levon.

'Grandad says it could be sooner.'

'How *is* your grandad?' asked Levon, offering Walter an apricot.

'Mum and Dad want to put him in a nursing home.'

'Maybe it's for his own good. You remember how he went wandering down by the river?'

'He was just going fishing! Can't my grandad go fishing without everybody saying he's crazy?'

'He had no fishing rod, it was the middle of the night, and he was wearing his pyjamas.'

Walter couldn't stop himself from smiling even if he wasn't sure why. 'You might be right,' he continued, 'maybe Grandad is unwell, but *maybe* there is something I can do to make him better. I saw a programme on TV about a boy who was blind and got his eyesight back, and a man who was in a wheelchair who ended up walking again.'

'What about that guy who bought your dad's Loomobile?' said Levon with a smirk. 'He *was* walking and he *almost* ended up in a wheelchair.'

'That's not funny,' said Walter, kicking a can to stop himself from laughing. 'It's true, but it's not funny.'

'OK "mister miracle worker",' said Levon, 'why not start by curing my leg so that I don't hobble any more. Then you can fix your grandad.'

'No problem,' said Walter. 'I'll just chop a bit off the good one and make it the same length as the other!'

'Doctor, doctor,' said Levon, laughing, 'I get a pain in my leg when I walk . . .'

'I've got a simple solution,' said Walter, picking up the thread of a joke he had heard a hundred times.

'Don't walk,' said the two boys in unison.

Just then Annie Zuckers appeared,

sauntering along on the other side of the road, lost in thought. She had a bag on her back, a snorkel thrown over her shoulder and a wildflower stuck haphazardly in her hair, which partly covered her smoky blue eyes. She smiled a distant smile as she passed by.

The boys smiled back, though Walter's smile was a shy one.

'She must have been snorkelling in the lake,' he said under his breath.

'She does it every morning,' replied Levon. 'She's a fanatic.'

'I'd be scared to go snorkelling. I even get nervous in the bath.'

'I heard that she's taken up karate as well,' said Levon, making quick-fire martial arts movements with his hands.

'Kung fu,' said Walter, correcting him, 'and she's very good at it, too. She won a gold medal at a competition last week.'

'You really like her!'

'Will everybody *stop* saying that!'

'Even just a little bit?'

'She thinks I'm a dork. She'd probably kung fu me if she got half a chance.'

Levon shook his head. 'I bet you my hamster she likes you, too.'

'Well, I'm afraid that I don't like your hamster,' said Walter with a cheesy grin.

Eno Tnaig Pets

Walter and Levon found two seats together near the front of the school theatre and sat down. The door opened and Annie Zuckers strolled in.

'Here comes the rich girl from the big house,' somebody muttered.

'You're late again, Miss Zuckers,' said Miss O'Connor, who was sitting at the back.

Annie tossed her wet hair from her eyes. 'Sorry,' she said, dreamily detached, and then she spun on the heels of her cowboy boots and found a seat just behind Walter and Levon.

'She's behind you,' whispered Levon, as the caption 'One Giant Step' appeared on the screen.

'Shh,' said Walter.

Miss O'Connor dimmed the lights just as the image of a rocket blasting off into space filled the screen.

'This is a film about Man's race into space,

about the dream to go where no man had gone before.'

Neil Armstrong descended the ladder to the moon, then Walter and Levon joined in as he said the famous words, 'This is one small step for Man, one giant leap for mankind.'

Annie Zuckers leaned forwards. 'Shouldn't it have been, "one small step for 'a' man?"'

'She's right,' said Levon. 'It should have been "one small step for 'a man'". It doesn't make sense otherwise. "Man" and "mankind" are the same.'

'I guess you're right,' said Walter, scratching his head.

'Don't forget to mention it to Neil Armstrong if you ever meet him,' said Annie.

'Don't worry,' said Walter, 'I won't!'

'Would you three please stop talking?' shouted Miss O'Connor.

'And give him my regards, too!' said Levon.

'That's it,' said Miss O'Connor, jumping to her feet. She pressed the 'stop' button on her remote control, walked to the light switch and turned the lights up full.

'Ah, Miss,' said Walter. 'The movie was nearly over.'

'Don't "Ah, Miss" me, Walter Speazlebud,' said the teacher as she whipped her glasses from her eyes and folded her arms. Even though she was petite and spoke in a thin, high-pitched voice, *nobody* messed with Miss O'Connor. 'If you remember correctly, it was you who asked me to show the documentary. Now, if you want to have a laugh with Levon or chat up Miss Zuckers, please do it outside of class time.'

The class erupted in a cacophony of hoots and whistles.

'You're dead, Speazlebud,' said Gary Crannick. 'I was having a nice snooze, now you've ruined it.'

'Spoilsport Speazlebud,' shouted Heather Hetherington, with a tear in her eye.

Walter wished he could just magically disappear, or be sucked out of the classroom window by a giant tornado.

'My dad said that the moon landing never

really happened. It was only pretend,' said Sarah Viola from the back of the class.

'My mum said the same,' said Evanna Goldenwoods.

'My dad said it really *did* happen,' said Aron Kelly, 'and anybody who thinks it didn't is an idiot.'

'My dad is not an idiot,' snapped Sarah Viola.

'Of course it happened,' said Walter. 'There are lots of photographs to prove it.'

'That only proves you're a space cadet, like your dad,' said Gary Crannick.

'Leave him alone,' said Levon.

'Why don't you just limp off, hoppedy,' said Crannick under his breath, just loud enough for Levon to hear.

Miss O'Connor clapped her hands. 'Can anybody tell me what NASA stands for?'

'Nickers And Smelly Armpits,' chirped Mike Snuddlidge.

'Snuddlidge,' snapped Miss O'Connor, 'I want you to write out the word "knickers" with a "k" one thousand times with a pink, day-glo marker.'

Snuddlidge's face turned a pale green.

Of course, Walter knew the answer, but he kept it to himself. He had had enough fun poked at him for one day.

'It stands for National Aeronautics and Space Administration,' continued Miss O'Connor.

'Aero-naughties?' piped up Gary Crannick. 'Like when an astronaut blows a fart inside the space capsule?'

'I said "Aeronautics",' said Miss O'Connor, with a 'don't push your luck' look in her eyes. 'A-e-r-o-n-a-u-t-i-c-s, the world of aerial and space navigation.'

'*Scituanorea*,' said Walter. He just couldn't help himself saying interesting words backwards. He did it without thinking.

'What's "astronaut" backwards?' somebody asked.

'*Tuanortsa*,' said Walter.

Annie Zuckers closed her eyes as if savouring the sound of the word Walter had created.

38

'Extraordinary?' she said.

'*Yranidroartxe.*'

'Concentration?'

'*Noitartnecnoc,*' said Walter. 'That's one of my favourites.'

'Supercalafragalisticexpeadalidocious,' said Mike Snuddlidge, sneering.

'*Suoicodilaepxecitsilagarfalacrepus,*' Walter rattled off, quick as lightning.

Mike Snuddlidge hissed.

'That's pretty amazing, Walter,' said Miss O'Connor, 'but I think we've had enough of your wonderful talent for now.'

'Yeah you should *tuhs ruoy ecaf,*' said Gary Crannick. 'My dad says that before dyslexia was invented people like you were just called stupid.'

Walter swallowed hard. Crannick's words were like a punch in the stomach.

'But people like you, Crannick, were always called ignoramuses,' snapped Miss O'Connor. 'You can tell your father that *I* said that.'

*

When the bell rang at the end of the day, Walter hung back, waiting for Crannick to leave.

'I've got to go, Walter,' said Levon as Walter helped him out of his seat. 'I've got physiotherapy for my leg in twenty minutes.'

'You mean you've got to leg it!' said Walter.

'I'll get you for that one,' laughed Levon.

'Why do you let Crannick talk to you like that?' said Annie as she walked past. 'You should stand up for yourself.'

'He's just jealous of you, Walter,' said Miss O'Connor as she tidied her desk. 'However, the more respect you have for your gift, the more respect people will have for you. Your gift is extraordinary, and it's yours. Maybe you just need to realise that. You don't have to spell backwards every time people throw words at you.'

Walter smiled. That was the thing he liked about Miss O'Connor – she wasn't one to hold a grudge.

'Miss O'Connor,' said Walter. 'You don't really think that the moon landing was faked, do you?'

'I don't know the answer to that question, Walter, but I do know that if you Google "moon landing" you'll find plenty of websites which support such claims.'

'I've seen those websites, Miss,' said Walter, 'but I don't believe them.'

'Sure, it's easy to dismiss such theories as crazy, but let me show you something,' said Miss O'Connor as she took an encyclopedia from her desk. She flicked through the pages to the 1969 entry 'moon landing'.

'Here is one of the official NASA photographs,' she said, showing Walter the famous shot of Buzz Aldrin standing on the surface of the moon with Neil Armstrong reflected in his visor. 'Many people say that it would have been impossible for Neil Armstrong to take such a well-composed, in-focus photograph of his colleague while bobbing around in zero gravity.'

Walter studied the photograph, which he knew so well.

'Here's another photograph,' said Miss

O'Connor. 'In this one the shadows on the lunar landing module seem to be going at different angles to the shadows of the rocks in the foreground. As the sun is the only light source on the moon it is hard to explain why this should be.'

Walter looked at the shadows. Miss O'Connor was right. The shadows were going in different directions.

'A lot of people believe that, whether they actually walked on the moon or not, the official NASA photographs were taken in a studio with professional lighting.'

'Maybe you're right,' said Walter, with a smile, but deep inside he *knew* that Man had landed on the moon and it would take a lot more than a photograph to make him change his mind.

A Yzarc Elat

When Walter returned to his grandad's bedside he found him sleeping once more.

'Cooome baaaack, Walter,' Grandad called out, but his eyes were still firmly shut.

Walter leaned over and tapped him lightly on the shoulder. 'Are you OK, Grandad? Are you having a nightmare?'

Grandad Speazlebud woke up in a tizzy. 'I dreamed you were on your way to the moon, Bartholomew!'

Walter reached into his pocket and took out a packet of Mrs Frost's Xtra Strong Mints.

'Ahh, suckers, I love suckers,' said Grandad with a slight lisp that made him sound like he was saying 'Zuckers'. This made Walter think of Annie Zuckers, and always made him smile.

Grandad popped a 'sucker' into his mouth and immediately his eyes brightened and his mind became clear again. 'Aah, perfume for the breath, tonic for the mind,' he said. 'Now, Walter, tell me all about the film.'

'I thought you were asleep when I whispered in your ear this morning!'

Grandad smiled mischievously. 'Nearly asleep and nearly awake.'

'Well,' said Walter, plonking himself down on the chair, 'it showed how the Americans and the Russians raced each other to be the first country to launch a rocket into outer space.'

'Aah, the space race,' said Grandad.

Walter nodded excitedly. 'And we saw Yuri Gagarin waving to the crowd before he became the first man *ever* to enter space.'

'That was 1961,' said Grandad.

'But it was the Americans who were the first to put a man on the moon –'

'In 1969,' said Grandad. 'And can *you* tell *me* the name of the crater in which they landed?'

'The Sea of Tranquillity,' replied Walter. 'And do you know how many astronauts have actually walked on the moon, including, and since, 1969?'

'Twelve,' replied Grandad.

He was right. And this is what confused Walter. Sometimes, Grandad's brain was as sharp as a razor, like now, yet other times he would forget what he had done that morning. There was one thing for sure – Mrs Frost's Xtra Strong Mints helped him to think, and though Grandad called them 'suckers', he never sucked a mint for more than ten seconds, then, CRUNCH, it was gone.

'Did you hear Neil Armstrong say his famous words?' said Grandad.

'That's a big step for a small man?' said Walter with a chuckle.

'That's very funny,' said Grandad. 'Where did you hear that one?'

'I heard it from you,' said Walter. 'That's your funny saying.'

'It is?' said Grandad.

Walter smiled and said nothing. How could Grandad forget that? Was he just pretending? Was he trying to be funny? He handed Grandad another mint, which he popped into his mouth, sucked and crunched.

'Grandad, do you think the moon landing really happened?'

Grandad Speazlebud took a deep breath, then gazed out of the window and into the distance, for what seemed to Walter like ages.

'Well, Grandad?' said Walter, the long silence making him uneasy.

'Did I ever tell you the story of the deer that went backwards?' asked Grandad, changing the subject.

'Of course,' said Walter, 'you said "**Reed**, **Reed**, **Reed**" and the deer went backwards across the road, narrowly avoiding the truck. But do you think the moon landing really happened?' Walter repeated. Maybe Grandad hadn't heard him the first time.

Grandad turned his gaze towards the photograph of his brother Bob Speazlebud with the Apollo 11 rocket in the background, and then he looked, once again, out of the window towards the sky, where a grey-tinged cloud was about to block out the sun.

'Have *you* any stories to tell *me*?' asked Grandad.

It was obvious that Grandad didn't want to talk about it.

'No,' said Walter wearily, 'just the story about the documentary.'

'Nothing strange happened today, did it? Nothing unusual?'

'No,' said Walter, 'nothing strange or unusual.'

'Nothing out of the ordinary?'

'No, Grandad. Why do you ask?'

But Grandad just closed his eyes and drifted back to sleep.

As Walter rose to leave, he looked for the red gemstone he had seen earlier that morning, but it wasn't there.

Annie Zuckers walked through the classroom door the next morning with her hair wringing wet and a devil-may-care expression on her face.

'You're late again, Miss Zuckers,' said Miss O'Connor. 'I often wonder why you don't just quit school and dive full-time?'

Annie smiled a dreamy smile and sat down.

Miss O'Connor took a newspaper cutting from her desk drawer. 'It seems that we will soon know the truth about the moon landing,' she said. 'This article from today's newspaper says that the Astralgazer telescope will soon be fully operational. The telescope will be powerful enough to spot the American flag *and* the footprints left by Neil Armstrong and Buzz Aldrin in the Sea of Tranquillity.'

She turned to Walter. 'I know that you collect cuttings about the moon landing, Walter. Would you like to take this?'

'Thanks, Miss.'

'Miss O'Connor fancies you, Spittlesuds,' said Gary Crannick.

'Hopefully, when we return on Tuesday morning, after the Bank Holiday,' continued Miss O'Connor, ignoring Crannick, 'the telescope will be operational, and there will be no more need for speculation. If the moon landing happened, scientists will see an American flag and two sets of footprints. If it didn't happen, there will be no American flag and no footprints.'

'I bet Tuesday's lunch that it did happen,' said Levon. 'Any takers?'

'Levon Allen, how many times have I told you this is not a betting office?'

'If it was all a fake,' said Evanna Golden-woods, 'those people who knew were pretty good at keeping secrets.'

'I agree,' said Miss O'Connor. 'I know I wouldn't like to carry such a dark secret around inside me all my life. I think I'd go mad.'

On Dadnarg

As Walter walked up the garden path after school, he had to shield his eyes from the glow of the fluorescent orange paint with which his mother had recently painted their house. Strangely, there was no music blaring from his mother's studio at the end of the garden. There was a simple equation when it came to his mum's paintings – the louder the music, the brighter the paintings. But no music at all simply meant she wasn't there.

He peered through the garage window, where he expected to see his dad working away on the Speazlebud Synchronised Suspension System, but there was no sign of him either.

Walter pushed open the front door. 'Mum? Dad?' he called, then he bounded up the stairs, two steps at a time, and knocked gently on Grandad's door. When there was no reply he turned the handle and crept inside.

His heart stopped.

The room was empty. Grandad was gone. There was nothing in the room but a folded note sitting on the bed. It was written backwards.

My dear Walter,
A bed became available at the nursing home
at short notice. I'm sad to leave this lovely
house and your wonderful company but
we'll still see each other; I'm just up the hill.
Lots of love,
Grandad.

Walter looked around the room, fighting back the tears. He noticed all the things that were no longer there: the old black-and-white photographs of Grandma on the wall, Grandad's walking cane, his hats perched like starlings on a telegraph wire, the books, the leather shoes arranged neatly under the bed, and all of Grandad's tablets and medicines.

Walter walked back downstairs, one heavy

step at a time. On the kitchen table he found another note. Wearily, he picked it up.

> *Dear Walter,*
>
> *I hope you read this note before you go upstairs. A room at the nursing home became available so your dad and I have taken your grandad there. I'm sorry it happened so suddenly but, as you know, there's a long waiting list for these rooms and we had to move quickly. I know you'll be disappointed not to have been here when he left. I've made your favourite dish – smoked haddock pie. It's in the refrigerator. Four minutes in the microwave should do it.*
>
> *See you soon.*
>
> *Love Mum.*

Walter walked towards the refrigerator, his mind racing and his stomach rumbling. He noticed that the door was half-open. He looked inside. Instead of a fish dinner, there was just an empty plate covered in hairs that looked suspiciously like the hairs of a ginger cat.

On top of the food cupboard, above the sink, he spotted a bushy ginger tail, quivering.

'*Ajaraham*!' he shouted, but Maharaja stuck to his hiding place.

'*Ajaraham*!' Walter shouted again, his anger building, but there was still no sign of Maharaja moving from his hiding place.

Finally, all the frustrations inside Walter's head ignited in one mighty thunderclap of anger. '*Aaaajjjjjaaaarrrraaaahhhaaammmm*!' he roared at the top of his voice.

Maharaja shot out from behind the cupboard, leaped athletically, backwards, on to the floor and reversed out through the cat flap.

'What was *that*?' exclaimed Walter, amazed. He glanced out through the kitchen window. The cat was now reversing across the lawn and leaping, with total disregard for gravity, backwards, up into the largest branch of the beech tree.

'*NOITANIGAMI*!!!!' he shouted. 'Grandad

wasn't making it up!'

Just then a bee flew in through the window and landed on his nose. It lifted its tail to reveal a needle-sharp sting, glinting like the sword of Zorro. Walter stared, cross-eyed, at the bee, then he said its name backwards, three times, '**Eeb**, **Eeb**, **Eeb**.' With that, the sting reversed back up into the bee's bottom, propelling the insect into the air where it zigzagged *backwards* around Walter's head, before reversing back out the window again.

When Walter's mum and dad walked through the door, they saw him standing there in a daze.

'Oh, Walter, I'm so sorry about Grandad,' said Peggy, throwing her arms around him.

'Grandad?' said Walter.

'Yes, *Grandad*,' said Peggy gently. 'He's gone to the nursing home.'

'Oh yeah, I know,' said Walter, realising that when two enormous events happen at once the first one gets blotted out by the second. He wanted to tell them about what had happened with the cat, but he couldn't. It wouldn't make sense to them. It barely made sense to Walter!

Harry looked at the empty plate on the table. 'You made short work of that dinner,' he said. 'You must have been starving.'

Walter smiled. 'I'm off to visit Grandad,' he said.

Na Noitativni Ot Levart

Walter ran up the steps of the Nittiburg Nursing Home and pushed through the old oak doors. As he walked down the hallway he was approached by a rotund nurse with a business-like manner and an angular visage. 'Can I help you, young man?' she asked sternly.

Her badge said, 'Nurse Hartnett'.

'I'm looking for my grandad, Arnold Speazlebud.'

'And you would be?'

'Walter. Walter Speazlebud.'

'Aah, **Retlaw Dubelzaeps**, the TV star!' she said, her coldness melting like butter in a pan. 'How could I not have recognised you? My granddaughter thinks you're very cute. Her name is Alison Conokin.'

'**Nosila Nikonoc**,' said Walter with a showman's smile. Despite what Miss O'Connor had said, he just couldn't stop himself. Spelling backwards was like a reflex to him.

'**Nosila Nikonoc**! That's what she calls herself!' said Nurse Hartnett. 'And where do you think you're going?' she suddenly shouted at a little old lady sneaking down the hallway.

'She's addicted to cheese,' the nurse said to Walter as the old lady scampered back to her room. 'I have to keep the fridge locked at all times.'

Ooh, thought Walter. *I wouldn't like to cross Nurse Hartnett!*

'Go on upstairs and take a right on the landing. Your grandad's room is number seventeen, first door on the left. The old codger is expecting you.'

Walter found the door open and his grandad sitting by the window. He stood for a moment in the doorway and glanced around the room. It was bigger and brighter than he had imagined, with a panoramic view of the surrounding Nittiburg Hills and the scent of summer blossoms wafting through the window from the garden. Grandad's books had been neatly stacked on the shelves, his hats were perched on top of the wardrobe, his photographs were hanging on the wall, and his shoes were by his bed.

'Walter!' said Grandad, looking up. 'Come on in.' He slowly stood up and embraced his grandson. 'You have something to tell me. I can see it in your eyes!'

'I can do it!' said Walter. 'I can do **Noitanigami**!'

'I'm so proud of you,' said Grandad. He looked like a great weight had been lifted from his shoulders. 'For years, without even knowing it, you have been preparing for this moment.'

'What do you mean?' said Walter.

'By being **Retlaw Dubelzaeps**! The ability to spell and speak backwards is the very foundation of the art of **Noitanigami**.'

'So making Maharaja go backwards wasn't a mistake?'

'In the world of **Noitanigami** there are no mistakes, Walter.' Grandad reached out and gripped Walter's hand, as tears welled up in the corners of his eyes. 'I've been waiting for this moment since the day I first heard you spell backwards. Now I know . . . that when I go . . . the power will be safe.'

Walter never liked it when Grandad said, 'When I go,' but as the evening sun lit the old man's face, he could see, more clearly than ever, the deep furrows that the passage of time had carved, and he knew that, as surely as the sun set, daily, over the Nittiburg Hills, his grandad's life was gradually moving towards its close.

'What power?' asked Walter.

'The power of **Noitanigami**,' said Grandad excitedly. 'Tell me what happened. How did you discover your power?'

'It was just like your story of the deer,' said Walter. 'When I accidentally said "Maharaja" backwards, three times, he reversed out of the door and up into his favourite tree. Then this bee tried to sting me and I sent him backwards, too!'

'They both returned to their last resting

place,' said Grandad. 'That's how simple **Noitanigami** works.'

'But where did the power come from?'

Grandad took a small, hand-carved wooden box from the bedside locker. He opened it to reveal the red gemstone sitting on a tiny blue velvet cushion.

'I saw that stone this morning,' said Walter. 'It was by your bed.'

'You must have touched it,' said Grandad, with a glint in his eye.

'I couldn't help it . . . there was something about it,' Walter admitted.

'Destiny is a powerful force,' said Grandad with a smile. 'I knew it was time for you to touch the Ruby Giftstone. It is the key which has unlocked your powers.'

Grandad handed the box to Walter and, as Walter looked at the stone, he felt his spirits lift, just like when he had first set eyes on it.

'When you touched the Ruby Giftstone you received seven gifts,' said Grandad. 'A "gift" in

Noitanigami is a single use of the power. When you have used all of your seven gifts you will be assessed by the Master and Keeper of the Ruby Giftstone.'

'Who's that?' asked Walter curiously.

'Me,' said Grandad.

'Wow!' said Walter. He never knew that his grandad was a *master* of ***Noitanigami***.

'And it's time for you to take over,' Grandad continued, 'to become the Keeper of the Ruby Giftstone and to inherit the additional powers that come with it – like the power to travel back in time. But to do so, you must *excel* in the use of your seven gifts. You must use them wisely and for the good of others.'

'Cooool!' said Walter. 'Can't wait to use those other five gifts!'

'It's not as easy as that, Walter. As part of your apprenticeship you must undertake a journey.'

'A journey?' said Walter.

'Yes,' said Grandad. 'You must travel back in time –'

Just then, Nurse Hartnett marched through the door. 'Are you filling your grandson's head with gobbledegook?' she said as she took Grandad's pulse.

'Are you being a nosy parker, listening to our conversations?' said Grandad.

Meanwhile, the words 'travel back in time' were still running around Walter's head. Could the power of **Noitanigami** *really* send him back in time? It seemed pretty incredible. But then again **Noitanigami** *had* sent the cat and the bee backwards, so maybe it *was* possible.

Nurse Hartnett 'accidentally' flicked one of Grandad's ears with her long red nails.

'Ouch.'

'I'll be back in ten minutes with a thermometer,' she said, as she headed for the door, 'and if you're not careful I know where I'll stick it – where the sun doesn't shine and where the birds don't sing!'

'What a woman,' said Grandad, his eyes twinkling.

'T-travel b-back in t-time!!' stuttered Walter. 'How?'

'You will be sent back in time by the Master, but *you* must choose the place and time you wish to journey to.'

Walter glanced at the table full of Grandad's medication.

Grandad read his mind. 'Don't worry. I can do it. I *must* do it!'

Walter swallowed hard. 'What if I get stuck back in time, Grandad?'

'Trust me, Walter.'

Walter looked into his eyes. Of course he could trust his grandad. He could trust him with his life, but his knees just didn't seem so sure. They were wobbling like jelly on a spoon.

Grandad coughed. 'But you might want to hang on to one of your seven gifts, just to be on the safe side.'

'What do you mean?'

'I mean that, even though you do not yet have the power to send yourself *back* in time, you do have the power to bring yourself home . . . in an emergency.'

'That's . . . good to know,' said Walter.

'So what do you say?'

'I . . . I'll think about it, Grandad.'

A Ykaerf Kcirt

The following day Walter and Levon sat by Nittiburg Lake, their fishing lines cast into the deep, still water.

'You can make things go backwards because you accidentally touched a gemstone?' said Levon with a chuckle. 'Very soon the men in white coats are gonna take you *and* your grandad away to the funny farm.'

'It's the power of **Noitanigami**.'

'Moita miggaw wha?'

'I'll show you. Throw your apple into the lake.'

'No way! I paid Mrs Green good money for that apple. And I had to listen to her talking about her favourite boy, **Retlaw Dubelzaeps**. She went on and on and on.'

'Throw it in. I bet I can bring it back just by using my **Noitanigami**.'

'And if you can't?'

'I'll buy you a full bag of apples.'

'Done deal, stoopid!'

'But if I *can* bring it back I win your black rabbit.'

'My black rabbit? No way!'

'OK,' said Walter, 'I win the apple *and* your chocolate bar.'

'You're on,' said Levon.

Levon threw the apple into the lake. It landed with a splash twenty metres from the shore.

Walter stared at the apple as it bobbed up and down. '**Elppa, elppa, elppa**,' he said.

With a 'sluurwhhoossh', the apple came straight out of the water and back into Levon's hand.

'Whoah!' said Walter, still amazed by his new powers.

'That's a f-f-ffreak-k-ky trick!' said Levon.

'It's not a trick,' said Walter, taking the apple from his friend's hand and biting into it. 'And what's more, when I have performed *Noitanigami* seven times, I become Keeper of the Ruby Giftstone, which means that I will have the power to send myself back in time.'

'Now that's *very* freaky,' said Levon.

'I'll tell you something that's freaky,' said Walter. 'As part of my training, Grandad – the Master – needs to send me back in time.'

Levon looked him in the eye. 'Your *grandad* wants to send you back in time? That's not just freaky, that's dangerous. You could get stuck back there and you'd never see Annie Zuck– I mean, your parents again.'

Before Walter had a chance to give Levon a good elbow in the ribs, a head emerged from the water directly in front of them. 'I like the sound of time travel,' said Annie Zuckers.

Walter took a sharp breath in. How much had she heard?

'Good luck on TV tonight. I'll be watching,' Annie said. Then she pulled her goggles down over her eyes and disappeared beneath the surface.

'Oh no!' said Walter. 'I almost forgot about the TV show. What time is it?'

Levon looked at his watch. '***Retlaw***

Dubelzaeps, it's *showtime*. Let's go. Your car will be waiting for you, sir. And on the way you can tell me how you did that trick with the apple.'

'It's not a trick. It's **Noitanigami**,' insisted Walter.

'If I can't pronounce it,' said Levon, 'how can I believe it?'

Walter smiled to the camera.

'Spell "essential" backwards,' shouted a member of the audience.

'**L-a-i-t-n-e-s-s-e**,' said Walter, without thinking.

The woman checked the piece of paper on which she had written the word backwards. 'Amazing!' she exclaimed.

'**G-n-i-z-a-m-a**,' said Walter with a smile.

'Say my name backwards, **Retlaw**, I'm Francie Disseldorf.'

'**Eicnarf Frodlessid**.'

The audience erupted with laughter.

'Alexander Trammelstow,' a young man called out.

'**Rednaxela Wotslemmart**,' replied Walter.

Levon, who was sitting in the front row, put his hand up. 'Gary Crannick is a cockroach from hell.'

'**Yrag Kcinnarc si a hcaorkcoc –**'

Walter stopped dead. Sitting in the back row was Gary Crannick.

'The alphabet backwards,' a woman shouted from the back row of the auditorium.

'**E-h-t t-e-b-a-h-p-l-a s-d-r-a-w-k-c-a-b**,' said Walter with a bored expression.

'That's wrong,' she shouted back, 'it's **z, y, x, w, v, u, t** . . .'

'If you already know, then why did you ask me?' said Walter.

'What's he doing?' shouted the producer in the control room. 'We're not paying him to insult the audience!'

Ignoring more requests, Walter said, 'I'm now going to perform a song for a very special person.'

He cleared his throat and began to sing:

'Ho Ynnad Yob,

Eht sepip, eht sepip era gnillac.

Morf nelg ot nelg

Dna nwod eht niatnuom edis . . .'

The producer tore his headphones from his ears and threw them on the ground.

'I think it's "Danny Boy" backwards,' said one of his colleagues.

'I don't care if it's the National bloomin' Anthem! He's supposed to be spelling words backwards, not singing songs and insulting my audience!'

In the Nittiburg Nursing Home, Grandad clapped and sang along at the top of his voice as a slightly bewildered Nurse Hartnett turned on her heels and left the room.

In the studio, all around Levon, the audience began to hiss.

'Walter, you're going to get fired,' Levon called out, while waving his hands to attract Walter's attention, but Walter's eyes were closed,

70

and his singing was getting *louder*.

> *'Eht s'remmus enog*
> *Dna lla eht sevael era gniyd*
> *Sit uoy, sit uoy*
> *Tsum og dna I tsum edib.'*

'Get off the stage, you dyslexic moron,' shouted Gary Crannick.

Walter stopped.

'Dyslexic moron,' Crannick repeated, now that he had Walter's attention.

Annie Zuckers, sitting at home staring at the TV, said, 'Don't let him get away with it, Walter!'

Walter fixed his gaze on Gary Crannick. **'Yrag Kcinnarc**, **Yrag Kcinnarc**, **Yrag Kcinnarc**,' he chanted angrily, under his breath.

'Dyslexic mor–' said Gary Crannick and he stopped, like somebody had just hit 'pause', then, like somebody had just hit 'rewind', he found himself jumping to his feet and reversing up the aisle.

Grandad sat up in his bed and shook his head. 'What are you doing, Walter? You're wasting your precious gifts!'

'Cut to a commercial break,' roared the producer. 'I don't know what he's doing, but I want that kid off the show, *NOW*!'

'I think you've just blown your TV career,' said Levon, following Walter to the exit. 'What did you do to Crannick? He went backwards!'

'**Noitanigami**,' replied Walter. 'Do you believe me now?'

A Wef Ssorc Sdrow

Later, Walter knocked on the door of Grandad's room.

'Come in, Walter.'

'How did you know it was me?'

'Your knock was the knock of a boy who is ashamed. There was no confidence in it.'

Walter slumped into the chair. 'I know, Grandad. I shouldn't have used the gift in that way. I just got so angry.'

'Anger and **Noitanigami** are a bad combination,' said Grandad firmly. 'It was reported on the seven o'clock news.'

'Oh, no,' replied Walter, covering his eyes with his hands.

'Thankfully the boy thinks that he was hypnotised. He had no idea what had really happened.'

'Phew, that was close.'

'Too close, Walter! You will never inherit the

Ruby Giftstone if you waste your gifts like that.'

'I'm sorry, Grandad.'

'You also used a gift earlier in the day if I'm not mistaken.'

'How did you know?'

'The Ruby Giftstone glows every time a gift is used. I hope it was a good deed of some kind.'

Walter's cheeks lost their colour. 'I was just trying to show Levon my **Noitanigami**. It was a kind of bet.'

'A bet,' said Grandad, shaking his head. 'Haven't I told you before that for every bet there's a fool and a thief. The fool is the bettor and the thief is the winner!'

'Yes, Grandad.'

Then Grandad pointed to the wall. 'I wrote this poem for you.'

Walter read it out loud, forwards.

'Gifts are given to a man,
To speed the plough of heaven's plan.
Never squander them to show

To loyal friend or jealous foe
That you are King.
Use your gifts for joy to bring
For every gift is God's on loan
Like every seed that was ever sown.
So go ye with these gifts of gold,
And yes, be brave, yes, be bold,
Remember, never compromise
Be always watchful, ever wise
Never use your gifts to shame,
Degrade, humiliate or maim.
For if you do, I'll say it twice
You'll know the cost, you'll pay the price
You'll know the cost, you'll pay the price.'

'You have used four gifts, so, now, you have just *three* left,' said Grandad.

'It's not very many,' said Walter.

'True, but it's how you use those gifts that matters.'

'I'll be careful from now on, Grandad, I promise.'

'I know you will,' said Grandad with a

smile. 'Now, have you thought about travelling back in time?'

'Yes,' said Walter, 'but I'm scared I won't make it back.'

Grandad reached out and took Walter's hand in his. 'Walter, I would never force you to do anything you didn't want to do.'

Walter smiled. 'I know,' he said. 'Grandad, there's something I want to know: why did you not answer me when I asked if you thought the moon landing had really happened?'

Grandad's expression became serious once again. 'Maybe it's time to show you something,' he said.

'What?' said Walter.

Grandad reached over, took a piece of yellow paper from his bedside locker and handed it to Walter.

'What's this?' said Walter, unfolding it.

'Read it.'

'*Oath . . . of . . . Secrecy . . .*'

'Ssh, Walter, we don't want Nurse Hartnett to overhear.'

When Walter finished reading the Oath of Secrecy his hands were shaking. 'It's dated 13 July '69, three days before the moon launch,' he said. 'Where did you get this, Grandad?'

'Bob dropped it in my house when he returned from America thirty years ago. I think he did it deliberately but he's refused to talk to me about it – or about anything else – since.'

'Are you saying that the moon landing . . . may not have happened?'

Grandad looked out of the window once more. 'I'm not saying anything because I just don't know, Walter, but I'd like to know the truth, wouldn't you? Wouldn't the whole world?'

'Hi, you two,' said Harry, walking into the room.

'We thought you might be here,' said Peggy.

'I let you down tonight,' replied Walter, slipping the piece of paper under Grandad's pillow. 'I'm sorry.'

'Let us down?' said Peggy. 'You were wonderful. And that rude boy! I was glad to see the back of him.'

'I'll never work in TV again.'

'You're twelve years of age, Walt, relax,' said Harry. 'You've done the TV thing.'

'Your dad's right,' said Grandad with a wink. 'You've been a **VT rats** for years. There are more important things in life.'

'Come on, Walter,' said Harry, putting his hand on Walter's shoulder. 'What can we do to cheer you up? How about a test-run in the Zoomobile?'

Walter had an idea. 'Will you take me anywhere I want to go?'

'You name it, kiddo.'

Eht Elibomooz Stih Eht Daor

Walter stood staring at his dad's new invention, gobsmacked, then he ran his hand along the edge of the all-glass door which, when closed, formed a large, orange-tinted glass bubble on top of a sky-blue, cylindrical frame. He touched the wheels with his trainers. 'It's great, Dad. Really fantastic!'

'All-terrain, four-wheel drive,' said Harry. 'In you get, Walt.'

Walter jumped into the passenger seat, which was made of hand-upholstered red leather.

'The seats are taken from a vintage Pontiac,' said Harry.

'Let me guess,' said Walter. '1967?'

'You've been spending too much time reading my *Vintage Classics* magazines!'

Walter looked through the roof of the bubble

at the pale evening sky. 'Why aren't all cars like this?' he asked.

'Maybe some day they will be,' said Harry, climbing into the driver's seat and turning on the all-electric engine with a tap of his toe on the footswitch. 'Now, where shall we go?'

'I want to visit Uncle Bob and Aunt Gertrude.'

'Uncle Bob! Are you sure?'

Walter nodded.

'OK, Walt, but don't expect him to be any friendlier than he was before. You know what he's like!'

As they headed out of the village, Walter noticed pedestrians stopping to stare, and drivers almost crashing their vehicles as they craned their necks to look at his dad's wonderful invention.

'It's turning heads already,' said Walter with a laugh.

'They might like the exterior,' said Harry, 'but it's what they can't see that I'm proudest of. Thanks to the Speazlebud Synchronised Suspension System, this baby goes on any type of terrain, from the rugged mountain top to the flat sandy desert. Have a look at the drawings in the glove compartment.'

Walter opened the glove compartment and removed a large piece of paper, which he unfolded.

'It's a suspension system built for the future,' said Harry.

'It looks complicated.'

'Wrong way around,' said Harry.

'It . . . still looks complicated.'

'Let me show you how good it is.'

Harry veered off the main road and down a bumpy, rock-strewn lane that would eventually take them back to the main road.

'It's as smooth as a hovercraft!' said Walter, exaggerating slightly, as the Zoomobile took each pothole and jutting boulder in its stride.

Walter wished that *he* had a Speazlebud Synchronised Suspension System. What with Grandad in hospital, people saying that the moon landing never happened, and being fired from the TV, he was on a bit of a rocky road himself!

Harry glanced across and saw Walter's scrunched-up brow. 'I know you miss having Grandad living at home, Walt. It's not easy for you.'

'Dad, did Grandad ever have any special powers when you were growing up? Was he a kind of wizard or anything?'

'A wizard? Not that I know! Though he *was* a fantastic storyteller. He'd mesmerise us with tales of how he'd helped the Incas build Machu Picchu, or how he'd gone stargazing with Galileo Galilei in Italy.'

Walter raised an eyebrow and allowed a smile to pinch his lips. 'Maybe he *was* a wizard.'

'Maybe, Walt,' said Harry with a wink. 'Maybe.'

Aunt Gertrude gave Walter and Harry a big hug when they arrived at the door, but Granduncle Bob barely even said hello. He seemed more interested in the Zoomobile parked outside.

'Is that your *new* invention, Harry?' he scoffed.

'It's called the Zoomobile.'

'Huh,' said Bob, shrugging his shoulders.

'You should get a proper job so you can afford a real car.'

Harry smiled. He knew Bob too well to be offended by his rudeness and his gruff manner.

Bob looked down at Walter. 'How are you getting on in school?' he barked.

Walter could smell strong alcohol on his breath. 'Very well. Yesterday I saw a documentary on the space race and the moon landing –'

'I don't want to hear about it.'

Walter was going to say, 'but you gave me my first telescope,' but what was the point? Even though a year had passed since Walter had last seen him, Bob hadn't changed: he was still the same angry old man. And even though he was younger than Grandad, he looked much older – he was overweight, his skin was blotchy and sagging and his remaining grey hairs had been dragged mercilessly across his head to hide his prominent bald patch.

Aunt Gertrude, on the other hand, was as warm and welcoming as ever, though she, too, had aged noticeably since Walter had last seen her, and her hair, which was now tied in a bun, was almost completely white. Walter wondered if living with Bob was making her old ahead of her time. 'Don't mind Mr Grump,' she whispered. 'You're both so welcome.' With that she hugged Walter for a second time. 'Now, why don't you both follow Bob into the sitting room, while I make some sandwiches.'

'I'll help you,' said Harry.

'Oh, that would be marvellous.'

As he followed Bob down the hallway and into the sitting room, Walter noticed that Bob was more bent-over than ever before. Walter looked around the room. There was the small fireplace, lit as always, even in the summer; a floral-patterned couch which almost matched the carpet like camouflage almost matches trees; two armchairs; a mahogany sideboard full of silver and a couple of wedding photos on the wall. He could never understand why there was no telescope, no books on aeronautics, no photographs of the moon landing – nothing to suggest that Bob was ever really interested in the world of space travel, and certainly nothing to suggest he had ever worked for NASA as an aeronautical engineer!

Walter sat down. Bob may have interrupted him in the hallway, but he was *determined* to get him to talk about the moon landing. 'As I said, I just saw this wonderful documentary about the space race and the moon landing –'

'Ooh, my back,' said Bob, placing his hand on his spine and avoiding the subject, as usual.

'Bob and I saw you on TV,' said Gertrude, coming through the door with sandwiches and tea.

'Bloody television . . .' grumbled Bob. 'There's never anything on anyway . . . and that spelling backwards . . . it can't be that difficult . . . anybody could do it . . . I could do it!'

Forcing a smile, Walter took a pen and a piece of paper from his pocket and handed it to Bob. 'You probably *can* do it,' said Walter. 'Just try writing your name backwards and, if you get it right, I'll give you a **Retlaw Dubelzaeps** backwards-speller certificate.'

Bob wrote slowly and carefully, as a drool of spit dripped from his trembling lip. Walter noticed that his hand was shaking, too. Bob lifted his pen and examined what he had written. 'There, I think that's it. There's nothing to it!' he said, handing Walter the piece of paper.

Walter looked at the blotchy squiggle on the page. It was impossible to make out what he had written.

'How did he do?' said Gertrude as Bob stared at Walter, wide-eyed with expectation.

Walter felt a sadness he couldn't explain. He felt like he wanted to reach out and give Uncle Bob the biggest hug he had ever given anybody in his life. 'Top of the class,' said Walter, then he signed the spelling certificate and handed it to Bob.

'Well done,' said Gertrude, leaning over and giving Bob a kiss on the cheek.

'You should be on TV, Bob,' said Harry, clapping Bob on the back. 'There's a vacancy, you know!'

Walter threw his dad a dirty look and when he looked back at Bob he saw that a proud smile had transformed his face. And for a moment, Walter could see the younger Bob whom Grandad had often spoken about. Happy Bob, likeable Bob.

'Milk in your tea?' said Gertrude.

'Goddammit, you know I don't take milk in my tea!' barked Bob, his smile quickly disappearing from his face.

'I was talking to Walter,' said Gertrude, gently patting Bob on the arm.

'Yes, please,' said Walter.

Harry threw Walter a look which said, 'It was your idea to come here, son!'

'Can I use your bathroom?' said Walter, after they had eaten.

'Of course. You know where it is,' said Gertrude.

As Walter walked upstairs he heard the voice of Levon whispering in his ear. 'Betcha Bob has a secret room. Betcha ya can't find it!' *Hmmm*, he thought, *Uncle Bob* did *look like the kind of man who could have a secret room, but it might be full of dead bodies!* 'If there's a secret room I'll find it. You bet I will, Levon Allen.'

Walter searched the landing ceiling for an attic hatch but couldn't see one anywhere. He even looked in the bathroom. There was only one place left to look now. He took a deep breath, then slowly opened Bob and Gertrude's bedroom door and crept inside. There was a door in the wall! He tiptoed across the bedroom floor and opened it. Aha, a staircase leading to the attic! 'You're a genius, Levon!' he said. He slowly climbed the stairs until he found himself in a large, dimly lit room. He felt around for the light switch, flicked it on and gasped.

In the centre of the room sat a brand-new telescope on a tripod, its barrel projecting through a skylight towards the darkening sky. On a desk near the skylight were drawings and paintings of famous astronomers, whom Walter immediately recognised – Copernicus, Kepler and Galileo – and charts of the moon and all its phases, and a map

of the Zodiac. Then something caught his eye –
silver-framed photographs sitting on a table in the
corner of the room. He tiptoed towards them.
There was the photograph that Grandad had on his
wall: Bob with his arm around his brother Arnold.
Another photograph showed Bob with his arm
around an astronaut Walter vaguely recognised –
he may have been from one of the early Apollo
missions, but he couldn't name him. One
photograph really intrigued Walter – it was one in
which Bob wore a chauffeur's cap and uniform,
and stood in front of a limousine.

Now more puzzled than ever, Walter shook
his head. *Uncle Bob, were you an engineer or a
chauffeur? And why do you have all this stuff in a
secret room?*

He walked towards the telescope. Above
him, the moon was rising in the sky. Walter put his
eye to the eyepiece. This was the most powerful
telescope he had ever looked through. He felt as if
he could reach right out and touch the surface of
the moon. He had another question running

around in his head, perhaps the biggest question of all: *Will the Astralgazer Superzoom find two pairs of footprints and a flag on that moon?* Walter couldn't wait to find out. He had to know the truth. But there was another way to find out the truth about everything.

Eht Gib Noisiced

'You went to visit Bob?' said Grandad as Walter pushed him in his wheelchair down Nittiburg Hill. He had just eaten a Mrs Frost's Xtra Strong Mint and his mind was glacier clear. 'How was he?'

'He was . . . the same as ever.'

'Did he mention my name?' Grandad asked hopefully.

Walter shook his head. The actual word 'no' might hurt his grandad's feelings. He really wanted to tell him about that photograph of Bob dressed in a chauffeur's uniform, and the telescope hidden in the attic, but he thought it might confuse him. It certainly confused Walter.

They stopped at Walter's favourite spot, the old wooden bench overlooking the village. The bench, which had won the National Bench of the Year Gold Medal for the past ten years, had been hand-carved by his grandad as a gift to Nittiburg village. On the bench seat he had carved roses, their buds bursting into blossom, while sunflowers decorated the arm rests, every petal and pollen-grain lovingly carved in microscopic detail. Elsewhere, butterflies and bumblebees dipped for nectar; and swallows dive-danced through the air.

Walter helped his grandad from his wheel-chair and, as they sat down, they heard the sound of hammering coming from the direction of Walter's back garden.

'That must be Dad starting on a new invention,' said Walter. 'The Zoomobile is finished.'

'Did he hear back from the zoo?' asked Grandad.

'They returned his letter. It had been cut into tiny pieces. They enclosed a box of matches and a tin of lighter fuel. The note said, "Go away, Harry Speazlebud, you are a danger to society".'

'Was he disappointed?' said Grandad.

'Disappointed??' said Walter, laughing. 'He sent them a thank-you note and a banana for the monkey!'

'That's what I love about my son,' said Grandad; 'he never gives up, and he doesn't care what other people think. He may never become a famous inventor, he may never become rich, but every single day of his life Harry Speazlebud does what he loves to do, so day after day his dream comes true.'

Walter handed Grandad another mint. 'Have your dreams come true, Grandad?'

Grandad's eyes glazed over. 'I remember when I was your age, I stood on this hill and looked out over the village. I looked at all those wonderful trees in the forest over there – chestnuts, spruce, poplars, redwoods, and sycamores. Then I thought about the people down in the village sitting around their tables having dinner, sitting in their sitting rooms talking, sitting in their parlours playing games, watching TV – and I decided there and then to turn these beautiful trees – the ones that had fallen in the winter storms – into chairs for them to sit on. Special chairs, each carved to fit the personality of the person who sat on it. And that's what I did all my life. When we follow our heart's desire, Walter, the path of life appears before us like a stairway to the stars. So, yes, Walter, my dreams have come true . . . all except one.'

'Which one, Grandad?'

'To be re-united with my brother,' he said, sadly.

Walter stood up and took a few steps forwards, and then he turned and faced his grandad. 'I've made my decision, Grandad. I've decided to travel back in time.'

'You have?'

'I want to visit Granduncle Bob in 1969, just before the launch of Apollo 11. I want to find out why Bob changed like he did, and I want to know what the Oath of Secrecy is all about, and I want to find out the truth about the moon landing.'

Grandad smiled and clasped Walter's hand tightly. 'That's the journey I had hoped you'd choose!'

But Walter had a question. 'Why have you never done it yourself, Grandad? Why have you never visited your brother back in 1969?'

Grandad gazed into the distance. 'I thought about it many times, Walter. But I have always stopped myself.'

'Why?'

'I guess . . . I was afraid of what the truth might tell me. Now I am old I am not afraid of anything – old age, dying, and I'm certainly not afraid of the truth, so I *could* go now, but my heart tells me that the journey is your destiny and not mine.'

Walter smiled, because deep in his heart he felt it too.

Grandad reached into his pocket and took out the small, hand-carved wooden box from which he removed the Ruby Giftstone. He placed the stone in the palm of his right hand, then he closed his hand around it and placed his left hand on the crown of Walter's head.

Walter felt a gentle pulse of energy running through his body, from the top of his head to the tips of his toes. He could see the Ruby Giftstone glow through his grandad's closed hand. Looking his grandson in the eye, Grandad spoke backwards.

'Do you, Walter Anthony Speazlebud, accept the challenge given to you in the name of **Noitanigami** by me, Arnold Patrick Speazlebud?'

'Yes,' said Walter.

'Will you promise to use your remaining three gifts thoughtfully and bravely, in the pursuit of the truth, and for the benefit of others?'

'Yes.'

'Will you try with all your heart to learn the craft and master the powers of **Noitanigami** so that you can be called the keeper of the Ruby Giftstone?'

'Yes.'

'Go then, in the name of **Noitanigami**. Travel well and come back safely.'

Grandad unclenched his hand, placed the Giftstone back in its box and returned it to his pocket.

Walter had that feeling people sometimes have before they embark on a long journey, or a holiday in an exotic location. It is the feeling you are no longer fully *here*, that a part of your spirit has already flown and awaits you at your destination.

'I have something else for you,' said Grandad, handing Walter a small black book embossed with gold lettering, which said:

Noitanigami

by

Arnold Speazlebud

'All you need to know about **Noitanigami** is here. This is your copy.'

'You wrote this, Grandad!' exclaimed Walter as he opened the book. The introduction was handwritten, backwards, in the form of a poem. He read it aloud, forwards:

'This gift so rare
Given to you
Can make a million dreams come true,
Can stop the arrow-head of time

And send it back, for you and yours
To do the things you might have done
To win the battles you might have won
To right a wrong, or simply be
A witness to Man's history.
When spoken with the power of truth
That nestles in the heart of youth
This gift will cast a blinding light . . .
Then every man will surely see
The power of **Noitanigami***.'*

'I want you to be here, sitting on this bench, ready to travel, at 10 a.m. tomorrow morning,' said Grandad. 'The Master will work his magic from the comfort of his bed after a good night's sleep.'

'How will you know when to bring me back?' Walter asked.

'In time travel through **Noitanigami** time is compressed. If I send you back in time, to arrive in Florida six days before the launch of Apollo 11, and bring you home at 8 p.m., Florida time, on the day the astronauts return to earth, you will arrive back here on the same day as you left. In fact, you should be back before dinner time.'

'I never like to miss my dinner,' said Walter with a grin.

'However,' continued Grandad, 'if you need to come back at any time, you may, by using any one of your remaining gifts. The important thing, Walter, is to use your gifts wisely and to endeavour to master the art of **Noitanigami**. It is these two points on which you will be assessed.'

'It's a long way to go, Grandad.'

'I bet that Neil Armstrong said exactly the same thing when he was asked to go to the moon.'

'But . . . I'm not an astronaut.'

'We're all astronauts in our way, day by day, stepping into the future – the great unknown.'

'I'm taking a big step for a small man!' said Walter with a smile.

'Aha,' replied Grandad, 'you might even be taking a giant leap for mankind. Just remember to keep one gift just in case . . . anything goes wrong.'

A Oreh On Erom

'I need to ask a favour,' said Walter to Levon as the two boys left Maples' sweet shop later that day. 'Can you visit my grandad at 9.45 tomorrow morning and give him these please?' He handed Levon the packet of Mrs Frost's Xtra Strong Mints that he had just bought.

'Where will you be?' said Levon.

'I'll be getting ready to go time-travelling. I'm doing it, Levon. I'm going back in time!'

'You're crazy!'

'Maybe, but it's something that I *have* to do. I'm going back to 1969, to when the moon landing happened.'

'Wow!' said Levon. 'That sounds *amazing*! I didn't know you could go back in time. Next you'll be telling me you can fly!'

'I can't. Grandad's sending me back.'

Levon stared at the mints he was holding in

his hand. 'These are the mints that help your grandad to think straight?' he said.

Walter nodded. 'But remember,' he said with a smile, 'they're for Grandad, not for you.'

'I wouldn't eat one if you paid me! They're horrible.'

Just then, Mrs Green walked by.

'**Olleh, Srm Neerg**,' said Walter.

'Hello, Walter,' she replied coldly.

'What's wrong with Mrs Green?' said Walter when she had passed.

'People read the papers,' replied Levon. 'Apparently Gary Crannick's dad is very angry about Gary going backwards. He nearly got knocked down crossing the road.'

'He called me a dyslexic moron!'

'He calls me "hoppedy", but I don't send him backwards!'

'I bet you would if you could.'

'If I had your power I would have done the same,' said a girl's voice.

Walter turned around. It was Annie Zuckers.

'I know you used the same power to make Crannick go backwards that you used on the apple down by the lake,' she said.

Walter was stuck for words and slowly going red in the face. He tried to change the subject. 'Are you going scuba-diving?'

'Are you going time-travelling?'

'I'm . . . I'm thinking about it, but Levon says I'm crazy.'

'Go,' she said, her smoky blue eyes widening as they stared into his. Then she spun on the heels of her boots and strode away.

'Walter,' said Levon, 'this time-travelling business only happens in books. I bet you my bluey grey kitten that it's not gonna work.'

Walter didn't answer. He seemed locked in a trance, hypnotised.

Levon waved his hand in front of Walter's eyes. It worked.

'I bet you my telescope that it will,' Walter said.

'But you love your telescope.'

'I know. Don't you love your kitten?'

'I've got nine more!' said Levon. 'Can't wait to win my telescope.'

'Can't wait to win my kitten.'

Just then, a car screeched to a halt by the kerb, the window rolled down and a boy stuck his head out. It was the same boy who had stopped Walter just a few days before. 'Disgrace!' he shouted. 'That's what my dad says you are! Can you spell *that* backwards, **Retlaw Dubelzaeps**?'

Walter stared at the kid. There was so much nastiness in those small beady eyes.

'**Taht**,' said Walter.

The boy stuck his tongue out, then popped his head back in as the car sped off, leaving a cloud of fumes in its wake.

'You're both dead this time. DEAD!' It was the unmistakable voice of Gary Crannick. He was crossing the street towards them. 'I'm gonna bash your heads together.'

'Use your **Noitanigami**,' shouted Levon, as the two boys jumped on their bikes. 'Send him back home to his mummy.'

'I can't waste any more gifts,' said Walter as they pedalled frantically down the street with Gary Crannick chasing alongside on the footpath, his legs stretching out like an Olympic sprinter, his arms swinging, powering him along, his eyes half-closed. He was giving it his all.

'WHACK!'

Gary Crannick hit Mrs Green's vegetable display with such force that the scene which confronted Mrs Green when she ran from her shop resembled that of a vat of cold minestrone soup poured over a moaning boy.

'He must have tripped over some *string* beans,' said Walter with a broad smile, as the boys looked over their shoulders, still pedalling away.

'I knew something would *turnup* to save our lives!' replied Levon.

'You won't forget about the morning – Grandad in the nursing home – will you?' said Walter as the boys stopped outside Levon's house.

Levon saluted. 'I'll be at Nittiburg Nursing

Home at 9.45 a.m. sharp, Commander Speazlebud. Good luck with your time-travelling!'

'I'm no Commander,' laughed Walter, 'but
you're definitely head of Mission Control.'

Eht Tsim Latrop

The next morning Walter sat on Grandad's wooden bench. Beneath him, the 10 a.m. train sounded its horn as it left for the city. On his lap was a rucksack containing summer clothes and a toothbrush, and in his hand was *The Book of Noitanigami*. The newspaper cutting Miss O'Connor had given him was his bookmark for the chapter '**Gniraperp ot Levart**'. He had read through it last night and, this morning, before leaving the house, he had performed all the recommended stretching exercises to prepare him for the journey.

He opened the book at the chapter entitled '**Tahw ot od Nehw Uoy Dnal**' and glanced through it. It was pretty simple: 'Take a few deep breaths to help you overcome any dizziness you may feel and *pray* that you've arrived at the right place, at the right time!'

Walter searched his pockets for a second bookmark. Aha! He found a piece of neatly folded paper in his pocket. He unfolded it. It was the detailed drawing of the Speazlebud Synchronised Suspension System. *Oops! I hope Dad doesn't need it*, he thought, as he carefully folded the drawing again and placed it at the back of his book.

Five minutes later Walter was still sitting on the wooden bench. Grandad had never been known for his time-keeping, but there was a little voice inside Walter's head, which sounded very like the voice of Levon, and it was saying, 'I bet this time-travel business ain't gonna work, cowboy. You'll soon be throwing your bag over your shoulder and heading back into town without a horse.'

But Walter's hands were trembling, and sweat drops were running down the ridge of his spine, because there was another voice – his own – telling him that something was about to happen, something that would change his life for ever.

*

When Levon entered Grandad Speazlebud's room he found the old man sleeping deeply.

'Excuse me.' Grandad heard a boy's voice call out to him through the swirl of stars and the trails of meteors that brightened the celestial dreamscape in which he was soaring, floating, towards a blinding white light.

'Excuse me, Mr Grandad Speazlebud,' repeated Levon, raising his voice. 'Today is a big day.'

Today is a big day, thought Grandad, thinking he had thought the thought himself. *TODAY IS A BIG DAY! I HAVE TO PERFORM **NOITANIGAMI**.*

He opened his eyes to see Levon staring down at him. 'Levon!'

'Walter asked me to come and bring you some –'

'What time is it?' interrupted Grandad. He glanced at the clock. 'I'm late!' Then he pointed to the locker. 'Could you pass me that black book, please?'

Levon handed Grandad *The Book of Noitanigami*. He was surprised that there was actually a book on the subject. *Maybe this time-travel business is going to work!* he thought.

'There was a time when I knew this stuff off by heart,' said Grandad, 'but my memory is not what it used to be.' He flicked through the chapters, **Levart fo dnim**, **Levart fo emit**. 'Ah, yes, **Levart fo emit**. Would you mind reading this for me, Levon?'

'Sure,' said Levon, taking the book. '*In time-travel* **Noitanigami** *the subject's full name is called in its normal, un-reversed form three times, while the location of the destination is clearly imprinted on the mind.*'

'When Walter was reversing the apple he said apple *backwards,*' said Levon, confused.

'Backwards spells are used for everything except time-travel,' replied Grandad. 'Because time-travel is not actually going backwards at all, it is shifting dimensions. Now, what have I done with that piece of paper? Can you see it, Levon?' He fumbled for a piece of paper where he had Uncle Bob's Florida address in 1969, along with the specific geographical coordinates.

'I think it's in your hand,' said Levon.

'Oh,' said Grandad Speazlebud as he held the piece of paper to his eyes and examined it carefully. Then he closed his eyes, joined his hands together as if in prayer . . . and fell asleep.

Levon tapped him on the shoulder.

'Whaaaaaaaaaaaa,' said Grandad, sitting up straight.

'You were just about to send Walter back in time.'

'Walter who?'

'Walter Speazlebud, your grandson.'

'You're my grandson?'

Levon shook his head.

'Any suckers?' said Grandad.

Now Levon was really confused. 'Excuse me?'

'Any suckers?'

'I have no idea where she is!' said Levon.

Grandad closed his eyes in frustration. 'Any suckers? Any suckers? Any suckers?' he repeated.

Just then, Levon noticed something

glowing brightly on the bedside table.

'I can't chew. I can only suck,' continued Grandad.

'Oh, I get it!' said Levon. 'You want a mint! I thought you said Annie Zuckers!' He reached into his pocket and took out a pack of Mrs Frost's Xtra Strong Mints.

'Aahhh, tonic for the mind, perfume for the breath,' said Grandad, popping a mint into his mouth. Suddenly the clouds in his mind seemed to evaporate and his eyes began to sparkle. He glanced, once more, at the piece of paper containing the address and coordinates. 'Walter Speazlebud, Walter Speazlebud, Walter Speazlebud,' he said in a strong, clear voice.

Levon saw the glowing object again. He leaned over to take a closer look. It was a red gemstone. It must be the one Walter had told him about!

'Job done,' said Grandad triumphantly. Then he fell back on his pillow, exhausted. 'Phew, that's taken more out of me than I thought!' he said. 'Twice as much.'

Levon pointed at the stone. 'Is that the Ruby Giftstone?'

'Yes. Did you see it glow?'

'Yes,' said Levon. 'Twice.'

'Impossible. It can only have glowed *once*,' said Grandad.

'I'd bet my black rabbit on it, Grandad Speazlebud,' said Levon. 'The Ruby Giftstone glowed *twice*.'

At breakfast that morning Walter had tried to tell Peggy and Harry where he was going and why. Peggy had smiled and given him a hug, while Harry had asked him to bring him back a present from 1969. But he knew that they didn't *really* believe him.

Now, as Walter sat on the carved bench, waiting for something to happen, he, too, wondered if this time-travel business was all just a figment of his grandad's imagination. With that, a small, translucent ring of mist came out of nowhere and moved steadily towards his bellybutton.

'It's the mist portal of **Noitanigami** just like it says in the book! It's happening!' he shouted.

Then, *whooooosh* he was gone, and all that remained was the small ring of mist, which soon disappeared like a child's breath on a frosty winter's day.

A Esirprus Ni Emit

Walter glanced down to check what he was wearing. Phew! He still had on his blue T-shirt, grey corduroys and black and red stripy trainers. At least he didn't have a flowery shirt with a pointed collar, like some of those teenagers were wearing!

Nearby, a radio played a song with a fast thumping beat and a lot of 'Sha, la, la's'. Miss O'Connor had once told the class that they had used 'Du-waps' in the fifties, 'Sha la la's' in the sixties, and that the seventies were all about 'Hey, hey, hey'.

Walter could scarcely believe it – it had actually worked – he was now back in the sixties! Good ol' Grandad!

An elderly man wearing sunglasses and a straw hat walked towards him with the aid of a stick. 'Good morning, young fellar,' he said.

'Good morning,' replied Walter. 'Are you . . . Bob?'

'I ain't no Bob! Winston is the name.'

'Sorry,' replied Walter nervously. 'I'm looking for Bob Speazlebud's house. He lives on Sycamore Street.'

'Aha, *Bob Speazlebud*, Florida's most famous chauffeur?'

'That . . . could be him!'

'He don't need no kids calling to his door, what with the launch of Apollo 11 about to happen an' all.'

Right place, right time! thought Walter. *It had all worked perfectly!*

'You're probably looking for an autograph from his boss, Neil Armstrong.'

His boss! thought Walter. 'No,' he said. 'I'm a relative. I've come to visit him.'

The old man raised an eyebrow. 'Where are you from?'

'Nittiburg,' said Walter.

'Never did hear of no Nittiburg.'

'It's a long way away.'

'How'd ya get here?'

'My grandad . . . dropped me here.'

'Well, he dropped ya on the wrong street.'

'He probably got mixed up.'

'You better be who you say you are,' mumbled the old-timer as he made a 'follow me' gesture with his chin. 'If not, the CIA will be on to you like a fly on to a dog turd.'

They walked together past the teenagers on the corner with the weird clothes, then waited for the brightly coloured old cars to pass before they crossed the street.

'This is Bob Speazlebud's place.'

'Thank you,' said Walter as the old man shuffled off, muttering under his breath.

Number 25 Sycamore Street was a modest, white, wooden house with a neat flower garden and a garage at the side big enough to fit a limousine. Walter opened the gate and walked up the footpath to the front door. He looked over his shoulder. The coast was clear. He rang the doorbell. When there was no reply, he rang again, and when nobody appeared he took a deep breath and slowly turned the door handle. It was unlocked. He pushed the door open and walked into the hallway.

The first thing Walter noticed was a fishing rod lying just inside the door, and two photographs hanging on the wall; the photograph of a young Granduncle Bob standing alongside Neil Armstrong, and a photograph which Grandad also had, of Bob with his arm round his brother. A newspaper, the *Florida Herald*, dated July 10 1969 sat on the hall table. 'Six days to go', screamed the headline. Beside the paper were some letters addressed to 'Bob Speazlebud, 25 Sycamore Street, Fort Pierce, St Lucie, Florida.'

'Right time, right place!' exclaimed Walter. 'You did it, Grandad!'

'Bob!' he called out, as he continued down the hallway past the stairs and through the open kitchen door. It looked like the Nittiburg 'Antique Emporium' – there was a mottled red Formica-topped kitchen table with tubular steel chairs, an old blue leather armchair, a gleaming chrome pop-up toaster and a marbled glass bowl lampshade hanging by chains from the ceiling.

'Bob!' Walter called out once again. He looked out through the kitchen window into the back garden, where a grey squirrel was jumping from tree to tree.

'So, we meet again,' said a voice.

Walter's heart skipped a beat. He turned around slowly. 'Annie! What are *you* doing here?'

'I was walking home from the lake when I noticed something like a smoke ring coming towards me. Next thing, I was sucked into it at the speed of light, and dropped in a strange house in America in the late 1960s, if that newspaper in the hallway is correct!'

Walter was totally confused. Why would Grandad send Annie Zuckers back in time without telling him? 'I . . . I don't know what to say,' he said.

'When I saw letters addressed to Bob

Speazlebud, I reckoned you'd pop up sooner or later, so I had a nap in the sitting room.'

'You don't . . . seem too worried,' said Walter.

'Worried? I *love* adventure.'

'Did you see Bob?'

Annie shook her head. 'Who *is* Bob anyway?'

'I'll explain everything,' said Walter, 'or, at least, as much as I can.'

Walter sat at the kitchen table telling Annie everything he knew, while Annie practised her kung fu, cutting down her imaginary enemies with a series of lightning-swift kicks.

'So, you've blown *four* gifts already and you have only three left?' said Annie inbetween kicks.

'Yep,' replied Walter sheepishly.

'And each gift allows you to use your **Noitanigami** to make something go backwards?'

'**Noitanigami** is not just about reversing people, like I did with Gary Crannick, or making the apple return to Levon's hand. It has many different uses . . .'

'Like?' said Annie.

'L-l-like . . . w-w-well . . .' stuttered Walter. 'I haven't actually read the full book yet . . . but I know I can use it to send myself home if, for some reason, Grandad can't bring me back.'

'Do your parents know where you are?'

'I told them, but I don't think they believed me. What about yours? What will they think when you don't come home?'

'They're playing golf all day,' said Annie, staring at the ground. 'If I'm not there when they come back they won't even notice . . .'

'I don't believe that.'

'Oh, let's not talk about my parents . . . just tell me how you think I got here.'

'I think it was an accident!'

'An accident?'

'Grandad's not well. He gets confused. Levon's job is to feed him special mints to clear his mind . . . so he'll remember to bring me home.'

'In other words I may be stuck here for ever?'

'No,' said Walter, nervously. 'If Grandad doesn't bring you back, I will bring you back after I've returned to claim the Ruby Giftstone.'

'And to claim your Giftstone you've got to do some good stuff with your **Noitanigami** *and* get home safely?' Annie said.

Walter nodded nervously.

'So, in other words we could *both* be stuck here for ever!'

With that the door swung open and a tall, good-looking man, wearing a black suit and chauffeur's cap, entered the kitchen. He stopped dead.

Walter recognised him immediately from the photographs. It was young Granduncle Bob.

'I hope I'm not disturbing anything!' said Bob.

'Don't call the police,' said Annie, holding a threatening kung fu pose. 'We're friendly.'

Bob raised both his eyebrows, his bright blue eyes sparkling with life. 'Karate or kung fu?' he said.

'Kung fu,' replied Annie.

'What's the difference?'

'Kung fu is on Tuesdays and karate is on Thursdays.'

'That's good to know,' said Bob, with a laugh, as he took off his cap to reveal a head of shiny, wavy black hair. He loosened his tie, plonked himself down in the armchair and turned to Walter. 'You look like a Speazlebud,' he said.

'I'm Walter Speazlebud.'

'I was christened Robert Speazlebud but you can call me Bob.'

Walter couldn't believe it. How could a friendly man like this turn into a grumpy old man like Granduncle Bob? 'Are you really Neil Armstrong's chauffeur?' he asked.

'Sure am. I've just dropped the Commander at the Kennedy Space Center.'

'This is Annie,' said Walter. 'She's my friend from school.'

'Friend?' said Annie. 'We barely know each other.'

Walter took a deep breath and chanced a smile at Annie. She smiled back. He breathed out.

'We're time-travellers,' said Annie.

'Time-travellers!'

'It's true,' said Walter. 'Arnold Speazlebud, your brother, is my grandad. I live in Nittiburg in the twenty-first century with my mum, Peggy, and my dad, Harry.'

Bob scratched his chin. 'Hmmm. I've got a little nephew called Harry. He's a happy and chatty kid – always making things.'

'Well, he's still making things, and he's still happy and chatty.'

'And you're a grumpy old man,' said Annie.

'Annie!' said Walter.

'Oops,' said Annie, 'but that's what you said!'

'Grumpy?' said Bob, curiously.

'I can't talk about your future,' said Walter. 'It's one of the rules.'

'Whatever you say, but tell me, how did you *time-travellers* get here?'

'My grandad – your brother – has the power of **Noitanigami** which can be used to travel back in time. I am the Master's apprentice.'

'The Master?'

Walter took his *Book of Noitanigami* from his pocket and pointed at the cover.

'**Noitanigami** by *Arnold Speazlebud*,' read Bob.

'The rules and the tools,' said Annie.

'Exactly,' said Walter.

Walter could see Bob looking more and more confused. 'My Master is your brother, Arnold Speazlebud. He sent me here, and Annie, too . . . but *that* may have been an accident.'

'An *accident*?'

'Yeah, well you see,' said Walter, 'he's . . . not very well.'

'Tell me this,' said Bob, putting his hand to his brow to check that he wasn't suffering from a hallucinatory fever, 'how do I know you're not just two vagabonds wheedling your way into my confidence before you burgle my house?'

Walter removed the newspaper cutting from between the pages of his book. 'I brought this with me from the future.'

'You're having me on!' said Bob, reading

the date at the top of the page.

'Cross my heart,' said Walter.

Annie looked across at the cutting. She recognised it as the one Miss O'Connor had read to the class. 'It's real,' she said.

Bob read the first paragraph aloud: '*The Astralgazer Superzoom telescope, which will soon be fully operational, will be strong enough to allow us to see the footsteps left on the moon's surface by Neil Armstrong and Buzz Aldrin*.' He looked at Walter excitedly. 'They made it to the moon! They walked on the moon!'

'Well . . . that's the other reason I'm here,' said Walter. 'Many people believe that the moon landing was actually *faked* . . .'

'. . . which means that *no* footsteps and *no* American flag will be found on the *surface*,' said Annie, emphasising certain words with high kicks, which caused Walter to take a few steps backwards for safety.

'Faked?' said Bob. 'Why would NASA want to *fake* the moon landing?'

'I have no idea,' said Walter, 'and neither has Grandad, but he really wants to know the truth before . . . before he . . .'

Bob raised his hand. 'No, Walter, there are certain things I don't want to know about the future, especially when they concern people I love.' He ran his fingers through his hair and took a deep breath. 'Me and my big brother . . . we may be oceans apart, but we're as close as two brothers can be. I'd do anything for him. Without him I would never have come to America. I would never have become an engineer for NASA. He encouraged me. He helped me to believe in myself. He helped me to believe in my dreams, and he did something that few brothers would do – he gave me the opportunity to go to college.'

'How?' asked Walter.

'You see, our parents had very little money. Yet they had scrimped and saved just enough to send one of us to college. Arnold was the elder. He did so well in his exams he could have gone, yet he didn't. He didn't go so I *could* go. He knew how much my dream meant to me. He even gave me some money so I could attend the most prestigious aeronautical school in the world. I owe it *all* to him.'

'You'll help your grandnephew, then?' said Annie.

Bob stood up and looked down at Walter. 'The question is, do I believe your crazy story? The answer is, I'm not sure. So let me ask you a question to check that you're for real. My brother – your grandfather – what is his career?'

'He's a woodcarver and furniture maker,' said Walter. 'At least he was until he retired.'

'And his hobby?'

'Fishing. I caught my first trout on his split-cane fly-rod.'

Bob glanced into the distance. 'What does his split-cane fly-rod look like?'

'It has a varnished cork handle with a sticker of a salmon jumping up a weir and –'

Bob reached out and placed both hands on

Walter's shoulders. 'You don't need to tell me any more. I believe you. I'll take you both as close to the action as I can. You'll see that there's nothing fake about the Apollo 11 mission.'

'Yessss!' said Annie, performing a high kick that missed the lampshade by millimetres.

'Tell me,' said Bob, 'did anybody see you coming here?'

'I met an old man called Winston,' said Walter. 'He showed me to your door.'

'Winston Pebbleby,' said Bob with a frown. 'He used to work for the Central Intelligence Agency. Now he's a busybody. Bad combination.'

'We're not doing anything wrong,' said Annie.

'Exactly,' said Bob. 'But if for any reason I feel it's best for you both to leave, then you've got to go. OK?'

Walter nodded while Annie pretended not to hear.

'Thanks for saying you'll help,' said Walter.

'I should be thanking you, kiddo,' said Bob. 'I've always wanted to do something for my brother, something that would allow me to show my gratitude for what he's given to me. Now you've given me the chance.'

Levon sat on the carved bench overlooking Nittiburg village and called out Walter's name. It echoed through the hills.

'He's gone!' he exclaimed. 'It actually worked!' But something didn't quite feel right, and he couldn't put his finger on it. One thing was certain, Grandad Speazlebud's mind was more than a little fuzzy. He might need another packet of Mrs Frost's Xtra Strong Mints. Levon stood up and stretched his bad leg. What concerned him most was not Grandad's confused mind, but the fact that the Giftstone had glowed *twice*. Why? And as he limped down the hill he could not, no matter how he tried, find a logical answer to that question.

'Nikibrotom

'I picked these up at the second-hand store,' said Bob, walking through the kitchen door and handing Walter and Annie a jacket each.

'And here,' he continued, reaching into the cupboard above their heads, 'are two spare helmets.'

'Why do we need helmets?' said Annie.

'We're going to the Kennedy Space Center on my Harley Davidson motorbike.'

'The Kennedy Space Center!' said Walter, barely able to contain his excitement.

'That's where Apollo 11 left from!'

'We're going to see the launch of Lunar Neptune 11, a test rocket replica of Apollo 11,' Bob said.

Walter gasped. A secret test launch? He had read about them but he couldn't believe he was *actually* going to watch one!

'Haven't they done all their tests already?'

said Annie. 'There are only a few days left before they go to the moon.'

Bob lowered his voice. 'There have been some hitches. As a precaution, NASA has ordered one more test. The eyes of the world are on Apollo 11, Annie, and the lives of the astronauts are in NASA's hands. Nothing can be left to chance.'

'Will they allow us in?' said Walter.

'No problem. I've just called my friends in security. I've said you're visitors from out of town.'

'More like, out of time,' chirped Annie.

'They didn't ask me which century you came from, so I didn't tell them,' said Bob with a wink.

'This jacket is a tight squeeze,' said Walter.

'And mine is too big!' said Annie, as her hands disappeared up her sleeves.

'Sorry, kids, we haven't got time to visit the tailor! Any questions before we go?'

'How did you end up as a chauffeur?' said Annie, boldly.

Bob sat down and joined his hands together as if in prayer.

Walter looked at him, anxiously awaiting the answer to the question he was too shy to ask.

There was a moment's silence before Bob answered. 'You see, in 1960 I began working as an engineer for NASA, and in 1967 I was appointed to the Apollo 1 mission, where I was responsible for the development of the Navigational Control System.'

'Apollo 1?' said Walter. 'Three astronauts died before Apollo 1 took off.'

'One of those astronauts,' said Bob sadly, 'was my closest friend, Gus Grissom.' He took a wallet from his jacket pocket, and from it produced a photograph. It showed Bob and Gus Grissom standing side by side. Walter recognised it immediately – it was the photograph he had seen in Bob's attic.

'It was Gus's dream that some day in the future the Apollo space programme would put a man on the moon.'

'Sorry about your friend,' said Walter, as Bob wiped away a tear that had escaped down his left cheek.

'I walked away from NASA that afternoon and vowed I was never coming back,' said Bob.

'But the fire on Apollo 1 was caused by a short-circuited wire in the cockpit,' said Walter. 'It had nothing to do with the navigational system.'

'True, Walter – you've been reading up – but I had seen how easily things can go wrong – how easily lives can be lost. Sending people into space is dangerous. One momentary lapse by an engineer can cause the death of an astronaut.'

'Remember the Space Shuttle Challenger,' whispered Annie to Walter.

Walter nodded as he remembered how one little mistake had cost so many lives in 1986.

'After that,' continued Bob, 'I rode my motorbike. I did a lot of fishing. I did a lot of thinking. But I missed the world of aeronautics. One day I got a call from Commander Armstrong. He needed a chauffeur, but he wanted somebody who was familiar with the world of aeronautics. He wanted somebody whom he could talk to about the world he loved.'

Bob paused, then continued. 'Deep inside I wanted to see Gus's dream come true. I wanted to be part of it. So I said yes.'

He opened the door for Walter and Annie. 'Now let me be *your* chauffeur.'

Eht Yknow Tekcor

Armed security guarded the entrance to the Kennedy Space Center as Bob's motorbike drew up outside.

'Hey, Bob!' said the security guard, handing him two laminated passes.

'Thanks, Victor,' said Bob, before handing the passes back to Walter and Annie.

'Have a nice day,' said Victor, waving them through.

Bob manoeuvred the motorbike through the gates and followed the signs to the launch area. As they drove past the famous glass-fronted Vehicle Assembly building, staff waved from their office windows and Bob waved back.

Walter pointed to a sign which said, 'Launch Pad 36A.' 'Annie, that's where Apollo 11 took off from on its way to the moon.'

'It hasn't happened yet!' she replied.

Walter, Bob and Annie stood on the elevated viewing platform of Launch Pad 35, along with a large group of NASA employees. All eyes rested on the majestic Lunar Neptune 11 rocket sitting on its launch pad, ready for take-off.

'It looks very small,' said Annie.

'It's just one-third the size of Apollo 11,' said Bob. He pointed to a small group of people sitting in a glass-covered viewing area. 'That's Commander Armstrong in the centre, Buzz Aldrin on the left and Michael Collins on the right.'

Walter gasped. Those tanned and smiling faces he knew only from posters and photographs were *actually* standing across from him! Bob waved and Neil Armstrong waved back. It sent a shiver up Walter's spine. Bob really *does* work for Neil Armstrong! This is *not* a dream! The astronaut waved once again.

'He's waving at you!' said Annie.

'No he's not!' said Walter.

'He is,' said Bob. 'I called him to tell him that

a big fan of his was coming to watch the build-up.'

Walter's knees trembled and his face went pink, but somehow he managed to pull himself together and wave back.

'Neil Armstrong looks nervous, too,' said Annie. 'I bet *he* never imagined he'd be face to face with the famous **Retlaw Dubelzaeps**.'

Walter gave her a gentle dig in the ribs.

'You can bet he *is* nervous,' said Bob. 'This is a big moment. This launch must go smoothly if the astronauts are to be confident that their lives will be safe.'

Annie pointed to some vultures circling high above in the deep blue Florida sky. 'Are those birds of prey trying to tell us something?' she said.

Bob laughed. 'They just want to watch the action, too!'

'If Levon was here,' said Walter, 'he'd probably say, "I bet something bad is gonna happen".'

'Don't say that,' said Annie, 'you'll put a hex on it.'

Walter smiled because, deep inside, he

believed Man had made it to the moon and left his footsteps in the sand. So, it was obvious – *nothing* was going to go wrong with the test rocket. *Nothing* was going to stop the Apollo 11 launch from happening. And *nothing* was going to stop Man from going to the moon.

The public-address system crackled into life.

'The countdown's about to begin,' said Bob.

'10 . . . 9 . . . 8 . . .'

Walter joined in the countdown as every cell in his body vibrated with excitement. '7 . . . 6 . . . 5,' he said, glancing at Annie and Bob – an invitation for them to join in.

'4-3-2-1,' they all chanted together. 'WE HAVE LIFT OFF!'

Lunar Neptune 11 took off in a convulsion of fire and smoke. The crowd cheered. The astronauts embraced each other. Walter, Annie and Bob clapped, whistled and punched the air with their fists.

Slowly, the rocket moved upwards in a perfect line, as if God was pulling it to the heavens on a piece of invisible string.

'Wow,' said Walter.

'Isn't that a sight?' said Bob.

'Cooooool,' said Annie.

Walter thought he noticed the rocket twitching, ever so slightly, and then leaning, just a little, to the left as it flew through the air.

'Should it be doing that?' he said to Bob.

'It's just a trick of the light,' replied Bob.

Walter glanced across at NASA's giant closed-circuit TV screen to see a close-up. The nose of the rocket was leaning more and more to the left.

'W-what's hap-p-pening, Bob?' said Walter, barely able to speak. 'It's veering off course!'

'I don't know, Walter!' said Bob.

'Houston, we have a problem,' said Annie, but neither Walter nor Bob smiled back.

The rocket had now turned almost ninety degrees and was flying parallel to the earth. Beneath the viewing screen NASA officials and engineers were running about in a blind panic.

Walter covered his eyes with his hands.

'You've got to do something, Walter,' said Annie, nudging him with her elbow.

'*What*?' he said, peeping through his fingers.

'Use your **Noitanigami**!'

'**Noitanigami**? I'm only a beginner . . .'

'And now's the time to begin, Walter! Where's your book?'

With one hand still covering his eyes, Walter fumbled in his pocket and took out *The Book of Noitanigami*. He opened the index. Three headings caught his eye.

'It must be one of these.' He read forwards, '*Reversing speeding objects, Reversing heavy objects, or Reversing faraway objects*. I haven't got time to read all that! I . . . I'll just try *something* . . .'

Walter took a deep breath and looked into the distance where the rocket was now just a small, faraway object weaving its way across the sky like a drunken aeroplane.

'**Tekcor**, **tekcor**, **tekroc**,' he said, using the most basic spell of **Noitanigami** while creating in his mind a picture of Lunar Neptune 11 returning to its base.

'What's Walter doing?' asked Bob.

'He's trying to reverse the rocket using his **Noitanigami**,' said Annie.

'It's not working,' said Walter, looking back at the screen.

'It's heading in the direction of the lakes,' said Bob. 'It's clearing the town of Waterville.'

'Try another one!' shouted Annie.

'**Rocket, tekcor, tekcor, tekcor, rocket, tekcor**,' said Walter, but the rocket continued on its wayward journey until it disappeared over the horizon and out of sight.

'I've a feeling it's going to end up somewhere near Lake Placid,' said Bob. His face was ghost-like but there was a sense of relief in his voice.

'Does this mean that Apollo 11 will be cancelled?' said Walter, still trembling from what he had just witnessed.

Bob put his arms around Walter and Annie's shoulders. 'Don't worry, the engineers will identify the problem and correct it. That's what these tests are for.'

'I told you I was just a beginner,' Walter said to Annie.

'At least you tried,' said Annie.

Walter flicked through his *Book of Noitanigami*. His eyes brightened as he pointed at a passage in the section entitled, '***Lareneg selur tuoba Noitanigami***'. 'At least I didn't waste a gift,' he said. 'Listen. *If the apprentice attempts to perform **Noitanigami** but fails, due to the use of an incorrect spell, the Ruby Giftstone will not glow, and a gift will not have been wasted.* I still have three gifts left!'

'I've a feeling you're going to need them,' said Annie.

A Elbirret Noitasilaer

'Have you seen Annie Zuckers around the village?' asked Mr Maple the shopkeeper as Levon entered the shop. 'She usually calls in around 10 a.m. every Sunday morning to pick up newspapers for her parents.'

Levon shook his head.

'I saw her going to the lake this morning on my way to work. What type of parents allow a young girl to swim on her own in a lake? I just hope she's OK. Now, how can I help you?'

'I want a packet of Mrs Frost's Xtra Strong Mints, please.'

'I tried one once,' said Mr Maple as he shoved a packet across the counter. 'Almost burned a hole in the roof of my mouth.'

'Same happened to me,' said Levon, handing over his money.

*

On his way back up the hill, Levon found himself thinking about what Mr Maple had said. Although he barely knew Annie Zuckers, he was worried about her. She didn't have any friends who Levon knew of, and her parents were known to play golf from morning to night, when they weren't flying around the world, so Mr Maple might be the only one to notice if she went missing. Like everybody else, he knew that the Zuckers lived in the walled-in red-brick mansion halfway up Nittiburg Hill, so he decided to stop by Annie's house just to see that she was OK.

'PRIVATE PROPERTY, TRESPASSERS WILL BE EXECUTED,' said the sign attached to the wrought-iron gate. It had originally said 'prosecuted', but the letters 'p-r-o-s' had been erased and replaced by the letters 'e-x'. Some blamed Gary Crannick but most people said that it was actually done by Frederick Hamilton Zuckers, Annie's multi-millionaire, globetrotting, yacht-owning, cigar-chewing, golf-playing father. And, they said, he meant it!

Levon pressed the buzzer and, as he waited for a reply, he wondered what kind of life Annie lived in that big house, the size of a castle, half-hidden behind trees, with no brothers or sisters to keep her company. *I bet a fat frog she's lonely*, he thought.

Then he remembered Grandad Speazlebud accidentally repeating her name this morning. 'Any Zuckers, any Zuckers, any Zuckers?' *That was funny*, he thought, smiling as he pressed the buzzer again.

Then he gasped. 'Oh no, Grandad Speazle-bud, we're in trouble! Now I know why the Giftstone glowed twice!'

He backed away from the gate and walked as quickly as his limp would allow up the hill to the nursing home.

A Dam Aedi

'Do you think they'll find the rocket?' said Walter to Bob and Annie, as they sat having lunch in the window booth of Dino's Roadside Diner.

'They have to!' said Annie, lifting her burger bun and squishing a dollop of tomato ketchup on to her barbecued double cheese burger. 'Time is running out.'

Bob glanced over his shoulder, and then whispered, 'Sure they will, and they'll correct the fault. Besides, you showed me the paper clipping. They went to the moon! I believe it. Don't you?'

Walter put his mouth to the straw and took an extra long suck of his large chocolate malt. He swallowed. 'Of . . . course . . . I do . . .'

'Isn't *she* pretty?' said Bob, distracted by the blonde, tattooed waitress in the short skirt who was passing by.

Walter glanced at her nametag. It said,

'Wynter Blossombloom'. He was hoping it might say, 'Gertrude'. 'She's OK,' replied Walter, 'but her name is weird.'

'I like her tattoo,' said Annie. 'She's got *style*!'

Bob laughed. 'She's into motorbikes, too.'

'So *that's* why you took your bike and not your limousine,' said Walter.

'Tryin' to impress the chicks?' said Annie.

'You two are cracking me up,' said Bob, as a newsflash appeared on the TV in the corner.

'Sshh,' said Walter.

'Today there is growing concern over whether or not NASA will be ready for the Apollo 11 launch. When pressed about the various tests they have been performing in secret, a spokesman said, "No comment."'

'If only we knew what went wrong,' said Walter.

'Telephone call for Mr Speazlebud,' Wynter Blossombloom called out from behind the counter.

'I wonder who that could be?' said Bob, sliding out of his seat.

He returned after a few minutes with a wide smile on his face, and an urgency in his voice. 'That was my friend Sammy, the warden of Lake Carrie, one of the smallest lakes in the Lake Placid area. He saw the rocket enter the lake!'

'That's a relief,' said Walter. 'At least nobody was hurt.'

'I've got to pass the information on to NASA,' said Bob. 'I *could* call them from here but, for the sake of security, it's better I tell them in person. We need to leave.'

Annie squeezed Walter's arm, then looked Bob straight in the eye. 'We've got to get there first.'

'What are you talking about?' said Bob, pulling on his leather jacket.

'Walter can reverse the rocket to the surface using his **Noitanigami**. I can dive beneath the surface and, Bob, you're an engineer – you can tell me what to look for.' Annie stared at Walter. She needed his support for her plan.

'Yyyeeeess . . .' he replied, 'I can *probably* reverse the rocket.'

'I have my goggles and wetsuit in my bag,' said Annie. 'I'm ready for action.'

'Are you both crazy?' said Bob, leaning across the table. 'Finding the rocket is NASA's job!'

'But *we* know where it is!' said Annie.

'Grandad says that if you want to find the truth you have to discover it for yourself,' said Walter, Annie's passion carrying him along like a tidal wave. 'That's why I'm here.'

Bob slicked back his hair and stared through the window at the cloudless evening sky. 'It's *very, very*, risky. In fact it's downright crazy.'

'Say yes,' said Walter. 'It's for your brother. You said you'd do anything for him *now* or in the *future*.'

'You did,' said Annie, raising an eyebrow.

Bob felt like a mouse cornered by a pair of cats. He looked at Walter, his green eyes full of expectation, and Annie, her blue eyes sparkling with excitement. Then Bob glanced over his shoulder to make sure that nobody was listening. 'I can't believe I'm saying this . . . but . . . *maybe* it's worth a shot – if you think you can do it, Walter. I did help to develop the Apollo navigation system after all, and I want to know the truth, too. But we're breaching NASA security, so we'd better keep it quiet.'

'Yesss!' said Annie as she took a coin from the table and jumped to her feet.

'Hey, that's my nickel,' said Bob.

'I'll take it as an advance for my services,' she said as she walked to the jukebox and punched in a number. She began a wild dance that turned the heads of every customer in the diner.

'She's a cool kid,' said Bob. 'That's one of my favourite songs.'

'You're cool, too, Bob,' said Walter. 'Much cooler than I imagined.'

'Why?' said Bob with a chuckle. 'Do I really end up as some grumpy old-timer with a beer belly?'

'If I answer your question I could fail my apprenticeship.'

'If you *could* give me an answer what would it be?'

Walter wasn't going to fall for that. 'We should be going,' he replied, changing the subject.

'Not before I get Wynter Blossombloom's number,' said Bob with a wink. 'For months I've been coming here trying to pluck up the courage to ask her out. If I can do something as crazy as this, I can ask a pretty girl out.'

'Don't get carried away,' said Walter, standing up to leave. 'One thing at a time, Bob.'

Gnivid Rof Seulc

Walter sat at the back of the speeding boat, reading his *Book of Noitanigami* in the glow of the setting sun.

'Learning anything?' said Annie with a playful smile as she kept an eye out for surveillance helicopters.

Walter looked up from his book. 'We'll soon find out,' he said.

Upfront, Bob steered the boat with the engine on full throttle. As they approached the orange buoy at the centre of the lake, Bob slowed the boat down. 'This is the spot where Sammy saw the rocket enter the lake.'

Walter put *The Book of Noitanigami* back into his bag and looked into the deep dark water.

'Look out,' shouted Annie, 'here comes a helicopter!'

'It looks like army surveillance,' said Bob.

'Cast out your fishing line, Walter.'

The helicopter swooped in and hovered above them, then moved off.

'We've got to act quickly,' Bob continued. 'Now show me how this **Noitanigami** works!'

Walter's hands were shaking.

'Take a deep breath,' said Annie.

'I'm not sure if I can do this,' said Walter.

'You *can* do it,' said Annie.

Walter gave a smile and nodded. 'I can do this,' he said to himself. 'Just follow the Master's instructions.' He reached out his hand, as the book had instructed him to, and pointed to the spot marked by the orange buoy. He closed his eyes.

'*Tekcor ala rocket ala tekcor ala rocket*,' he said, while clearly imagining the rocket slowly dislodging and rising from the bottom of the lake. He sensed a tingling sensation in his fingers. He raised his hand upwards and as he did he *felt* the rocket moving.

'There it is!' said Bob, as a fin of the rocket appeared momentarily, before settling just beneath the surface. 'That's some power you've got, Walter!'

'Well done!' said Annie. 'I knew you could do it!'

'You see,' said Bob with a smile, 'you're a natural **Noitanigamist**. Your grandad would be so proud.'

Walter blushed with pride. He could barely believe what he had just done. He had lifted a large rocket from the bottom of a deep lake. This was the *power* of **Noitanigami**!

Bob turned to Annie. 'It's over to you now, kiddo. You must locate the navigational control systems hatch. It's near the main fuel terminal hatch, two metres from the nose of the rocket.'

'Aye aye, captain,' said Annie, drawing her goggles over her face.

'The course corrector board is inside the hatch in a silver box,' Bob continued, looking around to make sure they weren't being watched. 'The coast is clear. Take care.'

'Good luck,' said Walter.

Holding her nose, Annie fell backwards into the lake.

Walter pressed the stopwatch button on his watch. 'She can hold her breath for three minutes,' he said.

'Let's hope that gives her enough time,' said Bob.

One minute and twenty-two seconds later, Annie re-surfaced. 'Got it,' she shouted, clutching the silver box. Bob grabbed the box and took it aboard.

'Uh-oh,' said Walter, pointing at the helicopter coming towards them.

'This is crazy,' said Bob. 'The place is crawling with security. We could all end up in jail.'

As Annie disappeared beneath the surface, to hide, Walter re-set his watch and cast out his fishing rod. 'We'll be OK,' he said, 'as long as it's not the same helicopter that saw us when there were *three* of us.'

'And as long as they don't see the rocket!' said Bob.

The helicopter came closer and hovered directly overhead, creating a powerful turbulence that whisked the water into a creamy foam.

'They'll never see the rocket through that,' said Walter.

Bob waved and mimed to show they were fishing. The pilot waved back, then whirred off into the distance. 'Phew,' said Bob, 'that was close. Too close.'

Walter's gaze stayed fixed on the helicopter. The man in the passenger seat looked very like the old man, Winston, who had shown Walter to Bob's house.

No! thought Walter, *it couldn't be*.

'Any sign of Annie?' said Bob.

Walter looked at the lake surface and then glanced at his watch. 'No, and she's only got ten seconds left!'

Five seconds later, at the stroke of two minutes and fifty-five seconds, Annie's head emerged, smiling. 'Five seconds left, am I right, Walter?'

'Amazing,' he said, shaking his head.

'Great work, Annie,' said Bob, helping her back into the boat.

'Merely a simple diving exercise,' said Annie. 'It's not exactly rocket science! Now, Mr Engineer, what's the problem with the rocket?'

'Give me a chance,' laughed Bob, retrieving the box from under the seat. He opened the panels with a screwdriver and removed the fuse board. 'Aha, just as I thought. The course corrector board was not connected properly to the fuse board.'

'Sabotage?' asked Annie.

'Bad soldering,' said Bob. 'This was an accident.'

'They'll find it, they'll fix it and go to the moon!' said Walter, with a look of joy and relief.

'No reason why not,' said Bob, as he closed the box and handed it back to Annie. 'One more time, Annie. This has to be returned to where you found it.'

Annie saluted, then she fell back into the water.

Walter reached into his bag and took out *The*

Book of Noitanigami. 'While she's gone I need to find out how to return the rocket to the bottom of the lake.'

'Hang on, Walter. We *want* NASA to find it now! We should leave it where it is.'

'Won't they think it's strange if they find the rocket floating?' said Walter.

'They'll be too concerned with finding out what caused the rocket to go off-course to bother trying to figure out why it's defying the laws of gravity,' chuckled Bob.

Srekcus Dna Srekcuz

When Levon arrived back at the nursing home, Grandad Speazlebud was sitting by his window, observing a pair of pigeons sitting in a tree. 'I love ducks,' he said, as Levon sat down with a look of grave concern on his face.

'I checked the bench on the hill,' said Levon gently. 'It looks like it all went to plan – you sent him back in time.'

'Who? What?' said Grandad.

'Walter, your grandson, he's not at the carved bench. I think it worked!'

'Oh, indeed, yes indeed,' said Grandad, but his voice still expressed his confusion.

'You *will* remember to bring him back from America, won't you?'

'Of course . . . bring back . . . Walter . . . America? What's he doing in America?'

'You sent him there!' said Levon in an

exasperated tone. 'You sent Walter back in time! Don't you remember?'

'I did what?'

Levon opened a packet of Mrs Frost's Xtra Strong Mints and handed one to Grandad. 'Grandad Speazlebud,' he said, 'don't you know where Walter is?'

Grandad popped the mint into his mouth. 'Of course I know where he is!' he replied. 'He's back in Florida in 1969.'

Levon breathed a sigh of relief. 'And do you remember me saying that I saw the Giftstone glowing *twice*?'

'Of course I do, and it made no sense at all. Still doesn't.'

'Annie Zuckers has gone missing . . . I think you've sent her back in time!'

'Should I call Nurse Hartnett and ask her to take your temperature?' said Grandad. 'You may be coming down with a brain fever, maybe Mad Cow Disease. When is the last time you had a dodgy steak?'

'I'm vegetarian,' said Levon, taking another deep breath.

'That figures . . . you look a bit pale around the gills . . . you need your iron, you know . . .'

'Please ask me if I have any sucking mints like you did when I arrived this morning.'

'This is a very silly game, Levon . . . Any Zuckers!' This time even Grandad could clearly hear how his 'S' sometimes sounded like a 'Z'. Suddenly, his expression changed from one of mild bemusement to one of extreme horror. 'This is a terrible mistake! In all my time as a *Noitanigamist* I've never sent an innocent bystander back in time. This is a disaster. We'll have to bring her home immediately!'

'We?' said Levon.

'Yes, Levon! I have already used two gifts in one morning. That's a huge drain on the *Noitanigamical* energies of an old man. I'll need your help!'

'But I'm not a *Noisybigamist*, or whatever it's called!'

'You may not be a **Noitanigamist** but page seventeen, chapter four in *The Book of Noitanigami* clearly states that a **Noitanigamist** can, if needed, call upon a Not**anigamist** for support in the execution of a **Noitanigami** spell.'

'I'm confused.'

'I often feel the same way myself,' said Grandad, 'and you can help your condition, and strengthen your concentration, by sucking a Mrs Frost's Xtra Strong Mint – perfume for the breath, tonic for the mind.'

'I can't eat those mints. No way. I've tried before. I just can't do it!'

Grandad cleared his throat. 'I . . . bet a box of Wilma Cartwright's Whipped Cream Fudge with Mango and Blueberry Bellies that you can.'

Levon wagged his finger. 'For every bet there's a fool and a thief, Grandad Speazlebud! Walter says that's one of your favourite sayings!'

Grandad pretended not to hear. 'How about two boxes? You'd be a *fool* to say no!'

'Two boxes of Wilma Cartwright's Whipped Cream Fudge with Mango and Blueberry Bellies?' said Levon. 'You're *so* on!'

Bob Seog Dam

'Bob's been gone a long time,' said Walter to Annie as they sat on the couch in Bob's sitting room the next morning.

'Let's watch the news to see if they've found the rocket,' said Annie, hopping up from the couch.

Walter pressed the 'on' button on the television in the corner.

'Good morning,' said the newsreader. 'NASA scientists are about to hold a press conference regarding the recent Apollo 11 tests. We can now go live to the Kennedy Space Center to talk to NASA spokesperson, Larry Spinatallone.'

A small, balding man in a smart navy suit walked on to the stage and took a sip of water. 'Good morning,' he said, then he coughed before continuing. 'NASA's top team of engineers have recently been carrying out last-minute tests in preparation for the Apollo 11 launch. We regret to say that our most recent test has revealed a mechanical fault with the fuel-level indicator.'

'The fuel-level indicator?' said Annie.

'That wouldn't cause the rocket to go off course,' said Walter. 'It's the course corrector board! They're lying!'

'Or else their so-called "top team" just couldn't find it,' said Annie, 'and they're covering up.'

'However,' continued Larry Spinatallone, 'engineers at NASA are convinced they can fix the fault. We are still on target to launch on 16 July. We *will* put a man on the moon.'

'If they send a rocket into space and don't know what the real problem is, it could be a disaster!' said Walter. 'Bob should tell them what we discovered before it's too late!'

The door opened and Bob walked in.

'We've seen the news,' said Walter, jumping to his feet. 'NASA's made a big mistake. They think it was the –'

'I want you kids to leave, NOW!' said Bob.

Walter was taken aback. He sounded just like

old Uncle Bob. What had got into him? 'But, Bob, don't we need to tell NASA what we found out?'

Bob ignored Walter's question. 'I should never have let you stay in the first place!'

Annie jumped to her feet. 'But they said it was the fuel-level indicator and not the –'

'Annie! Enough!' Bob shouted. 'I'm going upstairs to have a shower before I go back to work. When I come back down I want you both to be *gone*. Do you hear me? *Gone.*' He slammed the door behind him as he left.

'Has he become possessed by the devil?' said Annie.

Walter felt queasy. 'Did you notice a piece of paper sticking out of his pocket?'

'A piece of yellow paper?' replied Annie.

'It's an Oath of Secrecy,' said Walter. 'A promise that he won't talk about what's happening.'

'How do you know?'

'He left it behind at Grandad's house in 1969 when he came back from America. I've seen it.'

'Why would he sign a secrecy agreement *now*?'

'Maybe something is about to happen *now* that wasn't planned . . .'

'I don't like the sound of it one little bit, Mr Speazlebud. Let's get to the bottom of it.'

'No way! We're leaving!' said Walter. 'You heard what he said!'

'Are you crazy?' said Annie. 'Things are only *starting* to get interesting. The adventure is only *beginning* and –'

Walter interrupted. 'Annie, I'm going to use one of my two remaining gifts to return home. Then I'll ask Grandad to bring you back. Bob doesn't want us here!'

'Walter!' pleaded Annie. 'Don't run away now! This is our chance to find out the truth. To find out if Man really landed on the moon! Isn't that why you're here?'

Annie was right. His mission was to find out the truth. That was why his grandad had sent him here. He couldn't run away. 'OK,' Walter said. 'I'll go back right now, bring you home, then come back and lay low for a few days – see if I can find anything out.'

'Hang on right there,' said Annie, stamping her cowboy boots on the floor. 'We're in this together. We're staying and we're following Bob.'

'How?'

'We'll sneak into the boot of the limousine.'

'It's too risky.' Walter blushed. 'I . . . I don't want anything to happen to you.'

'I can take care of myself, *thank you*.'

'Sorry,' said Walter, 'I didn't mean to –'

'Your apology is accepted,' said Annie with a smile. 'Let's go.'

Levon made a crunching sound, then closed his eyes and swallowed.

'Now, that wasn't too bad, was it?' said Grandad.

Levon opened his eyes again. 'I did it!' he said triumphantly. 'You're right. I *can* eat a Mrs Frost's Xtra Strong Mint!'

'Don't forget to take your two boxes of fudge when you leave.'

'You bet I won't,' said Levon.

'OK, let's get to work,' said Grandad. 'On the count of three we say, "Annie Zuckers" three times. One, two, three.'

'Annie Zuckers, Annie Zuckers, Annie Zuckers,' they chanted together.

A faint brightness could be seen emanating from the Ruby Giftstone.

'That's not bright enough to make an ant go backwards,' said Grandad. 'One full packet, minus two mints, that leaves us with eight mints. Let's try half each.'

'Half . . . a mint?' said Levon, hopefully.

'Half of the *remaining* mints – four each.'

Levon groaned. 'Do I win anything if I eat four?'

Grandad shook his head. 'The bet was to see if you could eat a full mint. Now that you've eaten one, you can eat four or more, but I'll throw in a bunch of grapes and a creme egg . . .'

'You drive a hard bargain, Grandad Speazlebud.'

'Is that a yes?'

Levon nodded wearily.

Eht Elbaveilebnu Hturt

'Coast clear?' said Walter as Annie peeked round the corner of Bob's house and scanned the street. She turned and nodded as Walter pointed to a tiny mist circle that had appeared beside her.

'It's the portal of **Noitanigami**!' he whispered. 'Grandad's trying to bring you home!'

'I'm not ready to go yet,' said Annie as, to her relief, the portal faded, then disappeared.

'Let's go,' she said, dropping on all fours.

Walter followed her around the front of the house towards Bob's limousine.

Annie pressed the latch button on the boot. It popped open. 'Yesss!'

'Don't they lock anything around here?' said Walter.

'This is the biggest boot I've ever seen,' said Annie as she climbed in.

Walter clambered in after her and pulled the

boot shut. 'The back seats of these old limousines are collapsible,' said Walter in the darkness. 'We can get out that way.'

'Cool, so let's lie back and relax.'

'I'm taking off my jacket,' said Walter. 'It's warm in here.'

'Good idea.'

They soon heard the sound of Bob's footsteps walking towards the car.

'Sshh,' said Annie.

Bob opened the door, got into the car and started the engine. The car moved slowly out of the driveway, turned right down Sycamore Drive, left and left again, then accelerated as it hit the highway. After a while they veered off the highway, slowed down and then stopped. Bob got out. A few minutes later, two pairs of footsteps approached the car.

'Off to the studio, Commander Armstrong?' said Bob.

'Yes, Bob,' a tired voice replied.

'It's Neil Armstrong!' whispered Walter.

'Why is Bob taking him to a studio?' said Annie.

'Maybe they're doing interviews for TV.'

'We'll soon find out.'

The car came to a halt. They heard Bob talking to a security guard, then the car accelerated again.

'Here we are, Commander,' said Bob as he parked the car and applied the handbrake. 'The make-up truck is over there, rehearsals are on Stage One in twenty minutes.'

'Make-up? Rehearsals?' whispered Walter anxiously, as Bob and Neil got out of the car and walked away.

'We'll soon found out what it's all about, Secret Agent Speazlebud,' said Annie. 'But first we've got to get out of this boot.'

'You make us sound like spies,' said Walter, pushing the seats down and crawling into the back of the limousine, with Annie following behind.

'We're spies who seek the truth,' she said, peering through the darkened limousine window. 'Now, where did they go?'

'There,' said Walter, pointing towards a building with 'Stage One' written in large letters above the entrance. At the end of the building a man stood smoking a cigarette outside a door marked 'Exit'.

'Let's sit tight,' said Annie.

Minutes later, the man dropped his cigarette on the ground and went back inside.

'The coast is clear,' said Walter.

Annie opened the door and sprung into action, leading the way, head down, dodging between cars, until they reached the Exit door.

The door was slightly ajar. They slipped inside and found themselves beneath a bank of stepped wooden seating. Walter pointed to an opening between two rows of seats. They scuttled across and crouched down. The scene before their eyes made them gasp.

Walter felt as if he had just been hit by a bolt of lightning. Before him was a lunar landscape made of sand, scattered with small rocks, just like in the posters above his bed, and there, in the centre of the 'stage', was the lunar module – life-size, spectacular. Large movie lights bounced off huge umbrellas, giving the astronaut and the moonscape that 'studio' look Miss O'Connor had pointed out in those photographs she'd shown him. He tried to speak but no words came out.

Annie put her hands gently on his shoulders to comfort him.

To the side, in a chair marked Director, sat a man in a tweed suit smoking a fat cigar. 'Let's get the show on the road,' he called through his megaphone. 'I've got a party to attend in Hollywood tonight.'

The assistant director stepped out in front of the stage-set and faced the camera. 'Silence on the set,' he shouted. 'Take one . . . camera, and action!' He snapped his clapperboard then walked to the side of the set.

'I'm sorry, Walter,' said Annie.

NASA prepare to fake the moon landing. Note the
film camera and pulley at the ready.

'I'm so stupid!' replied Walter angrily. He couldn't believe that he was about to watch NASA *fake* the moon landing. It seemed that all those doubters were right after all.

'No, you're not. I believed they went to the moon too. So did most people in the world.'

An astronaut appeared from the lunar module and slowly climbed down the ladder to the 'moon' surface. He was attached to a thin wire connected to a spring-loaded pulley overhead.

Click! A camera flash illuminated the moment. Walter knew the image well. It was the official NASA photograph of Neil Armstrong about to set foot on the moon. The astronaut took one more step, bouncing up and down on the wire – a perfect simulation of walking on the atmosphere-free moon surface.

Neil Armstrong's voice could be heard through a speaker. 'This is one small step for Man, one giant leap for mankind.'

'Stop right there!' yelled the director. '"Man" and "mankind" is the same thing! What you mean is it's a small step for *"a man"* and a giant leap for *"mankind"*. Do it again.'

'He's an astronaut, not an actor,' muttered Walter angrily.

'Sshh. They'll hear us.'

'I don't care,' said Walter. 'I'm going to tell them what I *really* think.'

'Don't be stupid,' said Annie, grabbing his sleeve.

'Camera! Action! Apollo 11 moon landing, take two.'

Walter yanked his arm away and took off along the gap between the seats, towards the centre of the set. He stopped and faced the film crew. 'You're just a bunch of phoneys!' he shouted, 'and *you*, Neil Armstrong,' he said, turning to face the astronaut, 'how can you let them do this to you?'

The astronaut took off his helmet. It wasn't Neil Armstrong. It was an angry actor. 'Get off the set, kid. I'm just doing my job!'

'It's all a big lie!' screamed Walter.

'Security!' roared the director. 'Get this kid off the set, NOW!'

Bob, watching from the viewing area, dropped his coffee cup. 'What are you doing here, Walter?' he said under his breath.

Walter continued his rant. 'It's all just a lie!'

'You tell 'em!' shouted Annie, a proud smile now lighting up her face. 'You're crazy . . . but you're right!'

As two security guards ran towards Walter, Annie noticed something small and circular coming steadily towards her – a second mist portal!

'Leave me alone, you bunch of gorillas,' screamed Walter as the guards chased him around the 'moon'.

'Leave him alone,' shouted Annie, sprinting towards him and away from the mist portal, which momentarily seemed to follow her before tamely fading away.

'No, Annie!' said Walter.

But Annie kept coming. She leaped into the air and, with a lightning quick kick, she connected with the chin of the tallest security man, knocking him to the ground with a thunk.

Back at the nursing home, Levon shook his head in disappointment. The Ruby Giftstone, which moments earlier was bathing the room in a soft ruby light, had, once again, lost its glow – and they were clean out of mints.

But Grandad was more upbeat. 'We're getting close. I can feel it. We can't stop now, Pinocchio!'

Levon put his hand to his forehead. He knew what it meant – another trip to the sweet shop!

With a well-aimed movement of her knee, Annie brought the second security guard swiftly to the ground. 'Let's make a run for it!' she shouted.

'Put up your hands or we'll shoot.'

Annie looked over her shoulder. She was staring down the barrel of a gun. 'Maybe the gun is as fake as the moon landing,' she said.

'I wouldn't count on it if I was you,' said the armed policeman as Walter stopped running and pleaded, 'Do what he says, Annie.'

Bob stood there, helplessly looking on. *Walter, if they know we're connected I'll be fired. They'll throw me in jail. I can't do anything*, he thought.

'You too, boy,' the policeman shouted at Walter, as his back-up arrived. 'Put your hands in the air.'

Walter obeyed the order and, reluctantly, Annie did the same.

'You are both under arrest for conspiracy to spy.'

'We're not spies,' said Walter, 'we're –'

'That's enough, kid,' snapped a policeman, twisting Walter's arm behind his back and handcuffing him.

Annie looked across at Walter as she, too, was handcuffed. '. . . spies who seek the truth,' she said defiantly.

A Yrev Ssorc Noitanimaxe

'I'll ask you once more, punk. What's your name?' shouted Detective Crosscannon of the CIA as he stared across the table at Walter.

Officer Metalstone stood beside him, tapping her stubby fingers on the barrel of her gun. 'WHAT'S YOUR NAME?' she echoed with a throaty growl.

Walter glanced across at Annie, who sat beside him, cross-legged, looking bored.

'Willy Wonka,' he said with a grin.

Annie threw Walter a glance. She reckoned that Walter was being cheeky because they'd soon be going home, but what if they got stuck here?

Walter smiled back. He sensed Annie's concern, but he wasn't too worried.

Detective Crosscannon, sweat dripping from his forehead, placed his hands on the table. 'Are you both aware that you face charges of illegal entry into a high-security compound with the intention of spying on the activities of the National Aeronautics and Space Administration?'

'We're not spies,' interrupted Walter. 'We're –'

'Truth seekers,' said Annie.

Walter nodded.

'Now, let *me* give *you* some *truth*,' said Officer Metalstone. 'You are both facing imprisonment and, in addition to the spying charges, you, Miss, face a charge of assaulting two security guards.'

'They were attacking my friend.'

'Friend?' said Walter. 'We barely know each other.'

Annie elbowed him in the ribs.

'Ouch, that hurt.'

'Do you realise the seriousness of these charges?' said Detective Crosscannon, bringing his fist down firmly on the wooden table.

Walter leaned across the table and stared defiantly at the detective. 'They're not as serious as NASA *faking* the moon landing.'

Crosscannon's eyes looked like a pair of corn kernels about to pop.

Annie threw Walter a look which said, 'Be careful, Walter.'

Walter seemed unconcerned. 'Do you really think NASA will get away with it?' he continued.

'Nobody will *ever* suspect that the film footage they see on their TV screens next week is not the real thing,' the detective said. 'NASA have got the best director. This is watertight.'

'I'll make a bet that in the next century many documentaries and websites will claim that the film footage was faked,' said Walter.

'What the hell is a *website*?' said Officer Metalstone.

'A website,' said Annie, 'is information in cyberspace which can be read through a personal computer.'

'No one's *ever* going to own a computer except state agencies,' said Detective Crosscannon. 'Never. They're too big and too expensive. The government wouldn't allow it. And what are you, anyway – some kinda psychic who can predict the future?'

'You *could* say that,' said Walter.

The door burst open and a freckly young policeman stumbled into the room.

'Officer Sullivan, what have you got?' asked the detective.

'A Mr Winston Pebbleby has filed a report to the Police Department, saying that he met a boy who fits this young man's description. The boy allegedly said he was on his way to visit Mr Bob Speazlebud, ex-engineer at NASA, and now personal chauffeur to Commander Armstrong. The boy said his name was Walter and that Bob Speazlebud was his *uncle*.'

Walter swallowed hard.

'Hi, *Walter*!' sneered Detective Crosscannon, barely able to contain his joy. 'So you're related to Bob Speazlebud?'

'Mr Pebbleby also claims he saw the boy, Bob Speazlebud and an unidentified young girl on Lake Carrie, spying!'

'Oops,' said Annie.

'An inside job, eh?' said Officer Metalstone. 'Just what I thought!'

Levon arrived back with more mints.

'Good lad,' said Grandad. 'A full packet each just might do the trick.'

Levon grimaced. He handed one to Grandad, then stared at the packet in his hand like he was staring at a plate of soggy Brussel sprouts. 'I can't do it. I can't eat another one.'

'I bet a box of Wagonwheels, three plums and a pear I'll finish my pack first,' said Grandad, pretending not to hear.

'A bet?' said Levon, attacking the wrapper as if his very life depended on it. 'I bet a mouth organ and a goldfish I'll beat you to it!'

'Bob thought we had gone home,' said Walter to the detective.

'He told us to leave . . .' said Annie.

'Furthermore,' said Officer Sullivan, 'we

believe that these two travelled to the studio in the back of Mr Speazlebud's limousine. We found two jackets in the trunk.'

'Oops,' said Annie.

Walter shook his head.

Detective Crosscannon puffed out his chest. 'I think we've got enough evidence here to send them all to jail.'

'And throw away the key,' said Officer Metalstone, rubbing her hands together gleefully. 'Maybe *now* you would like to tell us your names and where you live, so that we can tell your parents that they'll never see their darlings again.'

'My parents haven't met each other yet,' said Walter.

'What are you talking about, you snivelly little lowlife?' said Officer Metalstone.

'We're . . . we're from the future.'

'I can't believe that this has happened,' said Neil Armstrong to Bob, as he sat restlessly in the back seat of the limousine. 'We were on the brink of one of the most important moments in history, and now I have to sit in a studio in front of a microphone saying "One small step for Man, one giant leap for mankind", while some two-bit Hollywood actor jumps about in a spacesuit, pretending to be me!'

Bob glanced in his rear-view mirror and saw the blank look of defeat in Neil Armstrong's eyes. He, too, felt ashamed because of the lie he would have to carry around inside him for the rest of his life. How would he face Arnold again – the brother who had believed in him, the brother who had encouraged him to follow his dreams?

Just then, a police siren snapped him out of his thoughts and a car with flashing lights pulled up alongside.

'Pull over!' a voice crackled through a megaphone. 'Bob Speazlebud, you are under arrest.'

Eno Tsal Ecnahc

'From the future?' tittered Detective Crosscannon. 'If you don't start answering our questions, I'll send you to the future *on the toe of my boot.*'

The door opened and Bob Speazlebud entered, accompanied by an officer.

'Bob,' said Walter as Bob sat down. 'I didn't mean to get you into trouble.'

'I didn't want you to know the truth,' said Bob, looking straight ahead. 'That's why I asked you to leave.'

'Blame me,' said Annie. 'I persuaded him to stay.'

'OK, that's enough *happy families*!' shouted Officer Metalstone. 'Walter Speazlebud, can you confirm that this man is your uncle?'

'Granduncle,' said Walter.

'Granduncle? He's not old enough to be your granduncle . . .'

'Walter is my grandnephew in the *future*,' said Bob.

'Future, SCHMUTURE! In *future* you should be careful of getting involved with spies,' said Officer Metalstone.

'Nice one, Metalstone,' said Detective Crosscannon, giving the officer a high five.

'You should have your own TV show,' sniped Annie.

There was a knock on the door. Officer Sullivan opened it.

Stanley Kutz walked into the room, his face red with anger.

'Time to show some respect,' said Detective Crosscannon. 'Mr Kutz is the Flight Director responsible for the Apollo 11 mission.'

Walter stood up and saluted. 'Congratulations, Mr Kutz, that's one small step in a movie studio. One giant cover-up for mankind.'

Annie put her hands over her mouth to stop herself from laughing.

'Sit down and shut up, both of you,' roared

Officer Metalstone.

Bob threw Walter a stare.

Walter nodded.

Ignoring Walter, Stanley Kutz stared angrily at Bob. 'You have betrayed NASA,' he said to him.

'What are you saying?' said Bob.

'I'm saying that maybe you're working for the Russians – trying to prevent us from going to the moon so that they can get there first. Acting as Neil Armstrong's chauffeur is a great cover for a spy and a saboteur!'

'Bob is innocent,' protested Annie.

'I don't know what a sabba toor is,' said Walter, 'but my uncle is no *spy*. Tell them the truth, Bob.'

Everybody stared at Bob. He took a deep breath to quell the anger inside him. 'You've got a test rocket with a fault you cannot identify, Stanley. Saying that you found a problem with the fuel-level indicator was just a cover-up.'

'That's ridiculous,' said Stanley Kutz, but his face betrayed a look of shock. 'How would you know, anyway?'

'Because *we* found the rocket *first* and discovered the real problem.'

'*Found* the rocket! What do you mean?'

'We got to Lake Carrie before NASA did.'

'See, they *were* spying!' said Detective Crosscannon.

Bob ignored him and continued. 'Walter used his **Noitanigami** to bring the rocket to the surface.'

'Annie dived in to retrieve it,' said Walter.

'And if you check with the sub-aqua team, who found Lunar Neptune 11 after us,' said Bob, 'they will confirm that they found the rocket floating near the surface, 750 metres due east of Lake Carrie harbour. If they look *again* they will find that the course corrector board was not connected to the fuse board.'

'Bob,' said Stanley Kutz, scratching his head, 'have you gone crazy? You expect me to believe that?'

'Stanley,' pleaded Bob, 'we both want to see a man walk on the moon. It's always been our dream, hasn't it? And it was the dream of our friend Gus Grissom. If you believe me, maybe it's not too late to save that dream.'

Stanley Kutz stared at Bob for what seemed like an age. 'The course corrector board you say, Bob?'

Bob nodded.

Stanley Kutz turned to Detective Cross-cannon. 'Check Mr Speazlebud's story with the sub-aqua team.'

'Mr Kutz, with all due respect . . .'

'Just do it!'

'You can do it,' said Levon aloud to himself, as he stared at his last mint. Grandad Speazlebud was still one mint behind.

Three sucks, one crunch and a gulp later Levon raised his hands in victory.

'Well done,' said Grandad, before swallowing his last mint.

Levon wiped his watering eyes. 'I have a good feeling about this, Grandad Speazlebud. I think we can get Annie back this time!'

'That's the spirit,' said Grandad. 'That's the spirit of **Noitanigami**. One, two, three!'

A pale-faced and bewildered Detective Crosscannon returned to the interrogation room. 'The coordinates are correct, Mr Kutz. The rocket was found floating near the surface at the exact location specified by Mr Speazlebud. Apparently the divers were mystified as to how a ten-tonne rocket could be found *floating*.'

'Walter,' said Stanley Kutz, spinning on his heels, 'you say it was your power that took the rocket to the surface. You made it go *backwards* . . .'

'Well . . . yes.'

Stanley Kutz turned to Bob. 'Where is your limousine?'

'Outside, sir.'

Then he turned to Detective Crosscannon. 'I would like permission for Bob Speazlebud to take me and his nephew to Launch Pad 35 at the Kennedy Space Center.'

Reluctantly, Crosscannon nodded.

'I'm not going unless Annie comes with us,' said Walter.

'The kung-fu expert? I don't think so,' said Stanley Kutz. 'I was there. I saw what you did to the security guards.'

'They were attacking my friend,' Annie declared hotly.

'I'm not moving an *inch* unless Annie comes,' said Walter.

Annie smiled.

Stanley Kutz looked at Crosscannon for his approval.

'OK,' said Crosscannon, angrily digging his hands into his pockets, 'but we must insist on a full police escort.'

'Then what are we waiting for?' Stanley asked.

Ranul Enutpen Snruter

Bob's limousine, escorted by a police convoy, arrived at Launch Pad 35 of the Kennedy Space Center. Four security guards descended on the car, opening its doors simultaneously. Walter, Annie, Bob and Stanley Kutz got out.

'Why does he want us back here?' whispered Annie to Walter.

'I think he wants to find out if Bob and I are telling the truth,' Walter whispered back.

Stanley Kutz turned to Annie and Bob. 'I want you both to go over there to the viewing area. Walter, you stay here with me.'

'Good luck,' said Annie to Walter as she followed Bob to the stands where, one day earlier, they had watched Lunar Neptune 11 take off.

Stanley Kutz pointed to the large viewing screen. 'On the screen you can see Lake Carrie. The orange buoy marks the spot where

Lunar Neptune lies.'

Walter nodded curiously.

Stanley Kutz folded his arms. 'I want you to bring the rocket back to base.'

'Bring the rocket back to base!'

'It's time to show us your powers. If you can, you may save the mission – Man *may* go to the moon. If you can't, you, Annie and Bob will be left to suffer your fate.'

Walter looked across at Annie, who was standing at the front of the viewing stand beside a puzzled-looking Bob. '**Noitanigami**,' he said silently.

Annie turned to Bob. 'He has to use his powers.'

Walter searched his pockets – he didn't have his book! He must have left it at Bob's. He looked up again to see hundreds of NASA employees filling the stands. Bob and Annie were shouting their support at the top of their voices. It was obvious they believed in him. *Now I must believe in myself*, Walter thought. *I must prove to Grandad that I deserve the Ruby Giftstone.*

Walter took a deep breath, then looked up at the screen and concentrated with all the power he could muster. But he didn't feel that surge of energy he had experienced at the lake. He didn't feel a tingle in his fingers. He felt nothing at all. He looked across at Annie. His eyes said it all. '*It's not working!*'

She stared back, her eyes lighting up like beacons. 'Believe,' she mouthed.

'I believe,' Walter said silently. 'I believe that Man will go to the moon, I believe in Grandad, I believe in **Noitanigami.** I BELIEVE IN ME!'

Gradually, Walter began to feel his power return, like a tickling feeling at the base of his spine. He turned away from Annie's hypnotic gaze and looked once more at the screen. '***Tekcor ala yks sky ala rocket,***' he said.

Immediately, the surface of the lake began to ripple. Then, *slowly*, the rocket emerged, like a monster from the deep, tail first.

Bob and Annie clenched their fists. 'Go, Walter, go!' they chanted. Stanley Kutz couldn't believe his eyes. The kid really did have special powers.

The rocket suddenly shot out of the water and up into the heavens, higher and higher, tracing a perfect arc in the evening sky.

'It's heading this way,' somebody shouted.

'How is he doing it?'

'He must have psychic powers!'

Walter relaxed his mind, slowed his breathing down and repeated the palindromic spell.

Some people began to run for cover but when they looked up again and saw Lunar Neptune floating gently towards the launch pad, they stopped in awe.

The rocket landed perfectly, without a sound.

Walter became aware of clapping, slow at first, then turning into a thunderous ovation. He turned and gave Annie and Bob a big thumbs-up. They were clapping too – their eyes welling up with tears of joy.

'Your grandad will be so proud,' shouted Bob. 'You really are a Master.'

Then Walter noticed Neil Armstrong. He was standing in the VIP stand, his eyes fixed on the rocket, his mouth wide open in wonder.

Beside Walter, Stanley Kutz had his mouth open, too. '*Extraordinary*,' he said to Walter. 'Bob was right. You *do* have powers.' He turned around and called out to a group of engineers standing nearby. 'I want somebody to check if the course corrector board has become disconnected from the fuse board.'

The chief engineer placed a ladder against the side of the rocket, ascended it and removed the silver box. Five minutes later, he emerged from the engineers' laboratory and walked nervously to where Stanley Kutz and Walter stood. 'Stanley, the course corrector board was *not* connected to the fuse board. We missed it last time.'

'That's the best news I've ever heard in my life!' said Stanley Kutz, throwing his arms around the engineer and lifting him into the air.

Bob and Annie had left the stands and were

walking over to Walter to see what all the commotion was about. As Annie came nearer, Walter could clearly see a mist portal following her. He was just about to run towards her, but before he did she was gone. She had disappeared into thin air! As the NASA employees were now running about excitedly, Bob was the only other person to see her go.

'What's happened to Annie?' said Bob when he reached Walter.

'She's gone home,' said Walter, with a look of deep disappointment. 'Grandad has brought her back.'

'Don't worry. You'll see her again soon,' said Bob.

Stanley Kutz put his arm around Bob's shoulder. 'You were right, Bob. Forgive me for doubting you. YOU WERE RIGHT!'

'Look behind you,' said Bob to Walter.

Neil Armstrong was standing there, grinning like a Cheshire cat.

'Commander Armstrong,' said Stanley Kutz,

'I'm so proud to introduce you to the boy who, along with Bob Speazlebud, has saved the Apollo 11 mission. This is Walter Speazlebud.'

'*Vice Commander* Speazlebud,' said Neil Armstrong, 'so nice to meet you.'

'V-v-v-ice C-c-c-ommander?' said Walter, nervously shaking his hero's hand.

'Indeed,' said Stanley Kutz. 'The astronauts *need* somebody of your talent.'

'I'll do anything I can to help,' said Walter.

'You don't understand,' said Neil Armstrong, putting both of his hands on Walter's shoulders and looking him directly in the eye. 'We want you to come to the moon.'

Neil Armstrong stared at Walter. Walter stared back. Had he heard him correctly? 'G-g-oing t-to the m-m-moon?'

'Young man,' said Stanley Kutz. 'For the safety of the astronauts, this mission needs you. If anything goes wrong you can bring the rocket back safely to earth.'

'Come with us to make history,' said Neil Armstrong.

Walter stood there, trying to make sense of it all. *What if something went wrong?* he thought. *I could be lost in space for ever*. He opened his mouth to say the word, 'No,' but as he did, he saw a picture of Annie in his mind. As if by magic, all his fear melted away. In his mind's eye he saw her standing there, whispering, 'Go, Walter, go.'

'What's it to be, Walter?' said Neil Armstrong.

Walter glanced at Uncle Bob and in Bob's eyes he saw his grandad looking back. Those eyes were saying yes, too.

Walter cleared his throat. 'YES, I will come with you to the moon.'

Neil Armstrong threw his arms around Walter while Stanley Kutz spoke into his walkie-talkie, 'Prepare one extra space suit – size small.'

A S'yad Gniniart

The following morning Walter jumped out of Bob's limousine with a bag on his back, and looked up at the tall glass building with the words 'NASA Training Center' written in silver above the main entrance.

'Good luck, Walter,' said Bob through the open window. 'I'm taking Commander Armstrong to his press conference. I'm dropping him off here after that. I'll pick you both up at six, then I'm off to meet Wynter Blossombloom.'

'The girl from the diner?'

'That's right,' said Bob, with a glimmer in his eye.

Poor Aunt Gertrude, thought Walter, *she's about to be replaced by a blonde bombshell and there's nothing I can do about it!*

'Enjoy yourself, Bob,' said Walter un-enthusiastically.

'You, too, kid. You're gonna have a ball.'

Walter turned to see Doctor Gordon waiting at the entrance. Walter knew his face from *The Encyclopedia of Aeronautics*. He was the head of Mission Control for Apollo 11, and he was carrying a chimpanzee.

'Welcome, Vice Commander Speazlebud. This is Loopy. He's been around the moon more times than the earth's been around the sun.'

Walter shook the monkey's hand. 'Hi, Loopy. Maybe you can give me a few tips!'

'No problem,' said the monkey, 'and maybe you can give me a few bananas.'

'Ahh,' said Walter, 'I saw your lips moving, Doctor Gordon.'

Doctor Gordon laughed. 'OK, Walter, time to start your training.'

'What's that?' asked Walter as they passed a glass-fronted showroom with a large go-kart-shaped automobile inside.

'That's the moon buggy. We hope to have it

ready for the next Apollo mission, but we're having problems.'

'What kind of problems?'

'The suspension – it's not springy enough for moon terrain.'

'The suspension?'

'Yes. We may have to abandon the project completely.'

'Dr Gordon,' said Walter, rooting in his bag and producing his dad's drawing, which was in the back of *The Book of Noitanigami*. 'Do you think that NASA would consider using the Speazlebud Synchronised Suspension System?'

'The what?'

'The Speazlebud Synchronised Suspension System – it will allow the moon buggy to glide like a hovercraft over even the roughest terrain,' Walter said in his best salesman's voice.

Dr Gordon put his reading glasses on and studied the drawings carefully. 'Fascinating and ingenious, Walter! I will make a photocopy and pass it on to Zlander Ovsky, the moon-buggy designer.'

Walter crossed his fingers. The new century didn't seem to appreciate his dad's genius, but maybe the last century just might!

Eybdoog Teews Dlrow

'We have lift off! History is about to be made!' said the headlines of the *Florida Herald*, as it sailed from the hands of the newsboy to the doorsteps of Florida.

Bob, dressed in his chauffeur uniform, was busily polishing the wing mirror of his limousine when a newspaper hit him on the head. He turned around and saw the newspaper boy cycling away and Annie Zuckers striding casually towards him up the path.

'You've made it back for the big day!' exclaimed Bob.

'What big day?' asked Annie.

Walter appeared at the front door.

'And there's the star of the show,' said Bob, 'ready for action.'

Walter couldn't contain his joy. 'Annie, you're back! What happened?'

'Well, first I landed in the rubbish dump. Then I went to visit your grandad to tell him you were OK. When he tried to explain *exactly* how I got here in the first place, he said my name three times – and here I am again!'

Walter laughed loudly.

'We should be on our way,' said Bob, adjusting his tie and looking at himself in the polished mirror. 'Let me just pop inside and get my Polaroid camera.'

'Where are you two going?' said Annie to Walter when Bob had gone inside.

'To the moon, Annie.'

'You're crazy.'

'You might be right.'

'Let's go,' said Bob, appearing again with his camera. He opened the back door of the limousine. 'Vice Commander Speazlebud and Miss Annie Zuckers, it's a pleasure to be your official driver.'

'Vice Commander?' asked Annie, following Walter into the back seat. '*What's going on?*'

'Neil Armstrong has invited me to go to

the moon,' said Walter proudly.

Bob handed Annie the *Florida Herald* as he sat in the driver's seat. 'You can hold on to this newspaper as a memento.'

She looked at the headline. '*We have lift off!*' she read. 'But we *saw* Neil Armstrong faking the moon landing! They're not going to the moon! They never *did* go to the moon!'

'You're partly right,' said Walter. 'They did *plan* to fake it but because of us, Apollo 11 really is going to the moon now, and I'm part of the crew!'

Annie's face went white. 'Isn't it a bit far from home?' she said, as the limousine rolled out of the gateway and down Sycamore Drive.

'I'm *already* far from home,' said Walter. 'What's an extra 384,000 kilometres?'

'I'm not talking to you if you're going to be a smart-arse.'

'Annie,' said Walter gently, 'when Neil Armstrong asked me if I would come to the moon I imagined you saying, "Go Walter, go". You do brave things all the time!'

Annie looked away. 'You might think that diving in a lake and fighting a couple of muscly morons is brave,' she said, 'but going to the bloomin' moon, with only *one* gift left. Now that's what I call crazy. CRAZY.'

'What would *you* have said if you were me?'

'I . . .' said Annie, turning her head, but not quite looking him directly in the eye, 'I would have said yes. Just be careful, Walter – *try* to hold on to your last gift. You *can't* rely on your grandad. Trust me on that one!'

Walter looked out of the window at the world passing by – he saw lean horses galloping through lush green paddocks, children playing on trampolines, an old man sitting on a deckchair in a flower garden, and in the blue sky above him an eagle hovering, stretching its talons as if sharpening them on the wind. Walter's gaze shifted once more to Annie's eyes, now smiling and sparkling again. He felt so alive, so much a part of this wonderful world . . . and he was about to leave it! He wished Grandad could call out across time and say, 'You're doing the right thing, Walter.'

Annie, seeing worry etched on Walter's forehead, touched his sleeve. 'Do what your heart tells you.'

Walter smiled. 'My heart is already halfway to the moon!'

Neil Armstrong kissed his wife and children goodbye and walked down the steps to the limousine where Bob stood holding the door open.

'Hi!' said Neil Armstrong to Walter as he sat opposite him. 'And you must be Annie,' he said, shaking her hand. 'You've made it back for the big day!'

'How do you know my name?'

'Walter told me a lot about you. You're part of the equation, Annie – an important cog in the wheel.'

Annie blushed.

'We spent the past three days at the NASA Training Center,' Neil continued. 'I got to know this guy pretty well.'

'Is three days' training enough?' said Annie. 'Don't you have to train for *years* to become an astronaut?'

'If an untrained monkey can survive for weeks in space, then this little monkey can survive for a week!' said Bob from the front.

'That's right,' said Neil Armstrong.

'Thanks a lot!' said Walter.

'That reminds me, Walter,' said Neil Armstrong. 'I believe you were a cheeky monkey when you were being questioned by Crosscannon and Metalstone.'

'Blame Annie,' said Walter. 'I was shy and quiet before I met her.'

'I don't think so,' said Annie, poking Walter in the ribs. 'You got fired from a TV show for sending a boy backwards when you should have been spelling backwards.'

'You can spell backwards, too?' said Neil Armstrong. 'Is there no end to your talents, young man?'

Now it was Walter's turn to blush.

'Buzz Aldrin?' Neil Armstrong said.

'*Zzub Nirdla*.'

'Michael Collins?'

'*Leahcim Snilloc*.'

'President Richard Nixon?'

'*Tnediserp Drahcir Noxin*.'

'You're a *suineg*.'

'And you're a quick learner, *Rednammoc Lien Gnortsmra*.'

'One full box of Mrs Frost's Xtra Strong Mints, please,' said Levon to Mr Maple.

'One full box! There are twelve packets in a box. That's a lot of mints for an old man!'

'I just hope it's enough,' said Levon dryly.

'Any sign of Annie Zuckers?' asked Mr Maple, placing the box on the counter.

'She's fine,' replied Levon. 'She had just gone time-travelling.'

'She's that kind of girl all right,' said Mr Maple with a wink. 'A bit of a spacer!'

*

'Good luck, Commander!'

'Be safe!'

'Take care!' people called out as the limousine drew up outside the Kennedy Space Center.

'This is what it must be like to be famous,' said Walter, seeing the faces pressed to the window, hoping for a glimpse of the Apollo 11 Commander.

'You *are* famous, **Retlaw Dubelzaeps**,' said Annie.

'It was never like this!'

'Would you rather be a public TV star or a secret astronaut?' asked Annie.

'I'd really have to think about that,' said Walter with a big grin.

A security guard checked Bob's documentation. 'Fine, Bob. Straight through and around the back. Launch Pad 36A.'

The limousine wound its way through the Space Center complex to the launch pad. Before them sat the magnificent Apollo 11 rocket, its nose pointing majestically to the heavens.

'Isn't she a beauty?' said Neil Armstrong.

Walter pinched himself. 'Is this really happening?'

'As real as it gets,' said Bob.

'As crazy as a dream,' said Annie.

Four armed security guards swooped on the limousine and opened the doors. Annie noticed a familiar face – it was one of the security guards she had kung-fued. He still had a black eye.

'Sorry about that,' she said to him. 'I was just trying to protect my friend.'

'We didn't know your friend was an astronaut,' he replied. 'We were just doing our job.'

'Well, you weren't doing it very well,' she said with a grin.

Dr Gordon stepped forwards. He welcomed Walter and Neil Armstrong and wished them both good luck. 'As you know, Vice Commander Speazlebud, your presence on this rocket must be kept top secret. You will change into your space suit and enter the rocket via the secret entrance tunnel at the rear. Commander Armstrong, you and your crew will say your goodbyes on national TV before following Walter onboard. We have one hour until lift off.'

A scrum of security guards marched towards Walter and stopped.

'Vice Commander Speazlebud,' said Dr Gordon, 'I've got somebody special for you to meet.'

'Is he another cog in the wheel?' quipped Annie.

'If he's who I think he is,' said Bob, 'he *is* the wheel.'

A guard stepped aside, allowing Walter to see the person they were shielding – a small balding man with dark bushy eyebrows.

'Mr President,' said Dr Gordon, 'let me introduce you to Vice Commander Walter Speazle-bud, the fourth crew member of Apollo 11.'

'I'm very happy to meet you, Walter,' said the President of the United States of America, reaching out his hand to Walter. 'By agreeing to accompany our astronauts on this historic trip you have shown strength of character and bravery beyond your tender years. I want you to enjoy your journey, and I want you to know that America will *always* be indebted to you. You are the dream-maker.'

'We're not there *yet*, Mr President,' joked Walter.

'That's true,' said the President, 'anything could go wrong.'

'That's not what I meant,' said Walter.

The President cleared his throat. 'I believe you claim to be from the future. Can you tell me one thing . . . have they invented a solution . . .?'

'For what, Mr President?'

The President looked around, and then dropped his voice. 'For hair-loss? I'm going pretty thin on top.'

Walter smiled sympathetically. 'I'm afraid people are still going bald in the future.'

'Mr President,' interrupted Anne, 'I'm Annie Zuckers and I'd like to shake your hand. That is, if you don't mind shaking the hand of a girl in this very *male* world of aeronautics.'

'Of course I'll shake your hand, young

lady,' he said, flashing a charming smile.

'I'm not a lady and I don't *ever* intend becoming one,' she replied, giving him a firm handshake.

As the President was whisked away, Dr Gordon tapped Walter on the shoulder. 'I want you to meet your fellow pilots. This is Lunar Module Pilot Buzz Aldrin Junior.'

Walter turned around to see the second most famous astronaut in history standing right in front of him.

'Glad to have you with us, Walter,' said Buzz Aldrin.

'P-p-pleased t-to m-meet y-you . . .' Walter stuttered.

'And this is Michael Collins, your Command Module Pilot.'

'You're a brave boy. Welcome aboard.'

The forgotten astronaut, thought Walter as he shook Michael Collins's hand.

'May I have your attention,' said Dr Gordon. 'I want astronauts Armstrong, Aldrin and Collins to go to the TV podium. Walter, please say your goodbyes and follow me.'

Walter had a sudden flashback to the first time he took the school bus on his own. He could see his mum standing on the side of the road, watching him climb the steps of the bus. As the bus took off, he turned around in his seat to see her waving, tears running down her face. That was just seven years ago. Now he was going to the *moon* and she didn't even know!

Sensing Walter's nervousness, Bob walked over and gave him a hug. 'You make me proud to be a Speazlebud,' said Bob. 'Enjoy the journey and come back safely.'

'What will you do while Neil Armstrong and I are away?' said Walter.

'I'm heading to the coast with my little lady.'

Annie raised her eyebrows.

'Wynter Blossombloom,' explained Walter.

'Annie,' said Bob, 'we'd love you to come with us. It's a good spot for diving.'

'That sounds wonderf–' She had just

glimpsed a mist portal. Walter saw it too and, although it faded without making contact, he sensed that the next one would be strong enough to take her home.

He threw his arms around Annie and gave her a big hug. 'If it wasn't for you, Annie, I'd be back in Nittiburg by now.'

'Bring me back something from the moon,' she said, giving him a kiss on the cheek, 'and try to hang on to your last gift. I want to see you again!'

'And when I get back I want you to show me how to dive.'

'It's a deal.'

Walter pointed to a second mist portal. This one looked like it really meant business. 'Tell Grandad I love him.'

She nodded, and then turned to Bob. 'I'm glad you didn't end up in jail, Bob.'

'I'm glad you didn't end up stuck in 1969,' replied Bob.

'It wouldn't be the worst thing in the world,' said Annie.

Bob handed her a Polaroid photograph he had just taken – of Walter talking to the President. 'So you'll know you weren't dreaming,' said Bob.

Then, *whoooosh* she was gone.

Og Ollopa Og

At 9.32 a.m. EDT on 16 July 1969, all round the world millions of people sat in front of their TV sets to watch the Apollo 11 countdown.

'10-9-8-7-6-5-4-3-2-1, we have lift off,' the voice said as the famous rocket slowly, amidst a fiery fury, left the ground, then sat momentarily in mid-air, before shooting upwards, leaving behind a vertical line of white smoke in the Florida sky.

'Are you OK, Walter?' asked Buzz Aldrin, floating into the cockpit.

Walter nodded. 'I can't help thinking about my grandad. If he could only see me now, floating around in my space suit on the way to the moon!'

'He'd be very proud of you, I'm sure,' said Buzz.

Walter smiled. 'He always said I could go to the moon if I *really* wanted to. I didn't believe him!'

Suddenly they felt a jolt and the sound of a small explosion, as the booster rocket fell away from the main rocket.

'You know, when I was your age,' said Buzz, 'I told my dad that one day I would be an astronaut and travel to the moon. You know what he said?'

Walter shook his head.

'"I don't just want you to *go* to the moon, I want you to be the *first man* to walk on the moon. I don't want you trailing behind somebody else. I don't want you to be second best".'

'But that can't happen,' said Walter, feeling sorry for Buzz. 'The Flight Commander has to go first!'

'I know,' said Buzz sadly. 'I know.'

Cinap Kcatta

Annie was still dusting dirt from her jeans as she walked through the door of Grandad's bedroom.

'You're back!' said Levon, jumping to his feet and waking Grandad from his nap. 'Hello, Annie.'

'Hello, Annie,' said Grandad, sleepily.

'We did it . . . again!' said Levon.

'We're the perfect team,' said Grandad.

'I feel like a bloomin' yo-yo!' said Annie.

'Where did you land this time?' said Grandad, as Levon helped him to sit up. 'Not in the rubbish dump again?'

Annie shook her head. 'This time I landed in the flowerbeds outside.'

'You see,' said Levon. 'We're getting better all the time.'

'Don't give up the day job,' said Annie sarcastically, as she spotted the pile of wrappers on the floor. 'How many mints did it take this time?'

'Six packets each,' said Levon.

'*You* ate six full packets of Mrs Frost's Xtra Strong Mints, Levon?'

'Perfume for the breath, tonic for the mind,' said Levon. 'The first five were the hardest. After that it was easy!'

'Erm, I've a feeling you're going to need some more,' said Annie. 'Walter has gone to the *moon*.'

'Gone to the *moon*!' said Grandad.

'He's got only one gift left!' said Levon.

'He said to say that he loves you,' said Annie.

'Me?' said Levon with a look of disgust.

'No,' replied Annie. 'Grandad Speazlebud.'

'Pheeeew,' said Levon.

Grandad sat up, joy brightening his tired eyes. 'He's *really* gone to the moon?'

'He's on his way. They've probably left the earth's atmosphere by now.'

'But you told us that the moon landing was being faked!' said Levon.

'There was a change of plan.'

'My grandson is on his way to the moon!'

said Grandad. 'How wonderful! How wonderful!'

'What are you talking about, Arnold?' said Peggy Speazlebud as she walked through the door. Grandad slid back down into his bed and tried to hide beneath the covers.

Peggy pulled them back and gave him a kiss. 'You're such a silly billy,' she said with a wide smile.

'Hi, Levon,' she said, turning around, 'so nice of you to visit Grandad. And you must be . . . Annie? We meet at last.'

'Hi,' said Annie nervously, as she shook Peggy's hand.

'So, where's Walter?' Peggy asked.

Levon and Annie looked at each other, then directly at the floor.

Confused, Peggy turned to Grandad. 'Where's Walter, Arnold?'

'Well, Walter . . . he went . . . I mean . . . I used my **Noitanigami** to send him . . . back to 1969 . . . and he got invited to go to the moon . . . and he's gone . . . It's my fault. I take full responsibility.'

'You're away with the fairies, Arnold! Maybe you need some of those strong mints to clear the cobwebs in your mind.'

'They're all gone,' said Levon, 'and so is Walter. It's true, Mrs Speazlebud, he's gone to the moon.'

'I've just come back from 1969, Mrs Speazlebud,' said Annie, passing Peggy the *Florida Herald*.

'*We have lift off! History is about to be made!*' read Peggy. Then she saw the date – '16 July 1969'. 'Why are you showing me this old newspaper?'

Annie then handed Peggy the Polaroid photograph showing Walter shaking hands with the President of America. 'That's Apollo 11 in the background,' said Annie.

Peggy put one hand to her forehead and, with the other, grabbed the radiator to steady herself. She turned to Grandad. 'Arnold, if this is *true*, you must bring him home *immediately*!'

'Who?' said Grandad.

'Oh no,' said Levon, 'the mints are wearing

off.' With that, he spotted a mint that had fallen on the ground. He picked it up, rubbed it on his sleeve and popped it into Grandad's mouth.

'Walter! Walter Speazlebud!' said Peggy. 'My son! Your grandson!'

'Vice Commander Speazlebud,' said Annie. 'That's his official title now.'

'I don't care what his bloomin' title is! He's Walter to me! He's my only child! He's my boy! Arnold, bring him back right NOW!' said Peggy fiercely.

Levon coughed nervously. 'Mrs Speazlebud,' he said as gently as he could, 'we can't bring him back right in the middle of the Apollo 11 mission. He's an astronaut now. It's what he's always dreamed of . . .'

Peggy flung her handbag on the ground and eyeballed Levon. 'Levon Allen, how would *your* parents feel if *you* were five thousand miles away, in another century, and on your way to outer space with three strange men!' Then she whipped around to face Grandad once again. 'NOW!'

'Peggy,' pleaded Grandad, 'he's a long, long way away. I'll need you, Levon and Annie *and* Harry to help me perform **Noitanigami** . . .'

'What is **Noitanigami**?' demanded Peggy.

'Let me show you,' said Grandad. 'I'll use **Noitanigami** to send you back home. That way you can tell Harry we need him.'

Then Grandad said, '**Yggep**' three times and Peggy disappeared, backwards, out the door. 'She should be back home in five minutes,' said Grandad.

'How come you didn't need our help that time?' said Levon.

'Simple **Noitanigami** is no problem,' said Grandad, 'but **Noitanigami** across time takes far more energy.'

'Maybe Levon and I should go for more mints,' said Annie.

'Great idea.'

'How many packs?' said Levon.

'I think we'll need one . . .'

'Only one?' asked Levon.

'One *wheelbarrow*,' said Grandad. 'One *big* wheelbarrow full to the brim of Mrs Frost's Xtra Strong Mints.'

'I know where there's a wheelbarrow,' said Annie. 'Let's go.'

Eht Elgae Sah Dednal

Neil Armstrong, Buzz Aldrin and Walter said goodbye to Michael Collins, then floated through the connection tunnel into the lunar landing module, the Eagle, and closed the hatch.

'Apollo 11 to Mission Control,' said Neil Armstrong. 'We're ready for the countdown to lunar module lift off. Over.'

'Roger,' replied Dr Gordon at Mission Control. 'Lunar module lift off has been cleared. All systems are GO. All lights are green. 5-4-3-2-1. Over.'

There was the sound of a small explosion as the lunar module detached itself from the command and services module, and began its journey to the surface of the moon.

'How do you get a baby astronaut to sleep?' said Walter. He often found himself telling jokes when he was nervous.

'Tell me, Vice Commander Speazlebud,' said

Neil Armstrong, as he looked through the window and saw the Eagle's shadow cast across the surface of the moon. 'How *do* you get a baby astronaut to sleep?'

'You rock-et,' said Walter.

The other two astronauts laughed.

'I've got one,' said Buzz Aldrin. 'Doctor, doctor, you've taken out my tonsils, my adenoids, my appendix, my gall bladder and one kidney and I still don't feel any better.'

'That's quite enough out of you,' replied Dr Gordon from Mission Control.

'Nice one, Doctor Gordon,' said Buzz as Walter and Neil broke into a fit of the giggles.

'Eagle to Mission Control,' said Neil Armstrong when his giggling had subsided, 'three thousand feet, descending steadily to the lunar surface. Over.'

'Roger, Commander. Expecting lunar module Eagle to land on target in the Sea of Tranquillity in approximately two minutes. Over.'

The astronauts looked down at the sandy,

rock-strewn surface beneath them. 'I just can't wait to take that first *giant* step,' said Neil Armstrong.

Smooth as an elevator stopping at the ground floor, the lunar module came to a halt. The three astronauts looked out of the window at the crater known as the Sea of Tranquillity.

With relief and pride, Neil Armstrong addressed Mission Control, 'Houston, Tranquillity base here. The Eagle has landed. Over.'

'Grandad,' Walter called out through time and space. 'I've made it to the moon!'

When Annie and Levon arrived back at the steps of the nursing home, pushing a large blue wheelbarrow full of mints, Harry Speazlebud was there to meet them.

'Hi, Levon, hi, Annie!' said Harry. 'Peggy is upstairs reading all about the amazing power of **Noitanigami**! It's all very exciting!'

'Aren't you worried . . . about Walter . . . getting home,' said Levon, out of breath. 'He has only one gift left!'

'One gift? He's the most gifted boy on the planet. Besides, he's never missed dinner in his life. He'll be back!'

Levon glanced at Annie with an expression that said, 'He's as loopy as Grandad Speazlebud.'

'OK, you two,' said Harry, 'we need to keep this operation from Nurse Hartnett. Apparently she's nuts.'

Luckily, Nurse Hartnett was on the telephone as they passed her office, Harry leading the way, and Annie and Levon crouching down while they pushed the wheelbarrow. But they didn't notice an open mint packet leaking through a hole in the wheelbarrow, creating a mint trail down the corridor, up the stairs and all the way to the door of Grandad's bedroom.

Ecafrus Noisnet

The three astronauts heard the voices of Mission Control whoop and holler in their earphones.

'OK, guys,' said Neil Armstrong, 'let's lower the lunar ladder and get to work. Walter, remember to stay away from the cockpit window. We can't let you be seen by my camera.'

'Commander Armstrong,' said Walter, as Buzz opened the hatch and began to lower the ladder.

'Yes, son.'

'I have a favour to ask.'

'Sure, son, you name it. Would you like me to bring you back some moon rock?'

Walter shook his head and took a deep breath. 'You see, Commander, Buzz's dad has always wanted his son to go to the moon.'

'Sure, and he's done his dad proud.'

'Yes, but his dad won't be happy unless Buzz is the *first* man to walk on the moon.'

'What are you saying, Walter?'

'I'm saying, please let Buzz go first.'

Walter imagined how Neil Armstrong must have rehearsed the words, 'This is one small step for a man, one giant leap for mankind', over and over again. He knew that he was asking a huge favour. He expected him to say, 'No.' It would take an extraordinary man to say 'Yes.'

'Walter Speazlebud, Walter Speazlebud, Walter Speazlebud,' repeated Grandad, Harry, Peggy, Levon and Annie. They glanced at the Ruby Giftstone. It showed only a very faint glow, barely enough to create even the wispiest circle of *Noitanigami*.

'OK,' said Grandad. 'Let's focus our minds on Walter. We must "see" him returning safely to Nittiburg Hill. One, two, three.'

'Walter Speazlebud! Walter Speazlebud! Walter Speazlebud!'

'If it's your wish, Walter, Buzz can go first,' said

Neil Armstrong. 'We wouldn't be here if it wasn't for you.'

Walter could barely believe it! He turned to Buzz and clapped him on the back. 'Good luck, comrade.'

'What can I say . . .' said Buzz. 'Thanks to you both. I'll never forget this.'

Buzz Aldrin placed his foot on the first step of the ladder, then, *whooooooooooosh*, he disappeared into space.

'What the?' said Neil Armstrong. 'The step has just broken!'

'Oh nooo!' cried Walter, as he watched Buzz floating away into the black void.

'It's time to use your **Noitanigami**, Walter,' said Neil Armstrong.

This was it, the moment Walter had dreaded. He would have to use his *very last gift*. Just then he noticed something round and misty coming towards him. It was the portal of **Noitanigami**!

'No, Grandad!' he shouted. 'Don't bring me back now!'

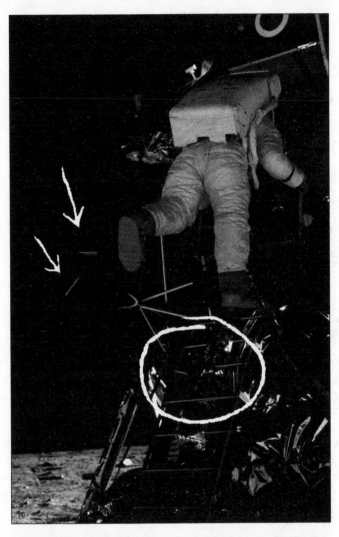

Buzz Aldrin began to drift into space just moments
after the step of the lunar ladder (highlighted) broke.

But the portal wasn't strong enough to penetrate the space suit and, with a sigh of relief, Walter watched it disappear. Then he focused on the floating astronaut and concentrated deeply.

Back at Mission Control, Dr Gordon used a five-second picture-delay to cut from the shot of Buzz Aldrin stepping on to the ladder, to a shot of the moon's surface. Nobody, except Mission Control, would know that Buzz Aldrin was floating in space, and nobody at Mission Control seemed too concerned.

'Walter will have Buzz back in no time,' said Dr Gordon.

'*Zzub Nirdla, Zzub Nirdla, Zzub Nirdla,*' repeated Walter, but Buzz Aldrin wasn't coming back.

'He's travelling deeper into space!' said Neil Armstrong. 'What's wrong, Walter?'

'Maybe my power is weakened by zero gravity,' said Walter. 'I'll need your help, Commander.'

Back at Mission Control, Dr Gordon was now looking very nervous. 'Come on, Walter,' he pleaded through his microphone. 'Perform your **Noitanigami**! Do your thing! That's why you're there!'

'Tell me what you want me to do,' said Neil Armstrong to Walter.

'Say the words, "**Zzub Nirdla**", with me, and "see" Buzz coming back. On the count of three – one, two, three.'

Walter was momentarily distracted by another mist portal. He took a deep breath. Once again it bounced off the space suit and disappeared.

'What's that?' said Neil Armstrong. 'Somebody blowing smoke rings in outer space?'

'My grandad's trying to take me home. We have no time to waste!'

'One, two, three, **ZZUB NIRDLA, ZZUB NIRDLA, ZZUB NIRDLA**,' they shouted together, so loudly that the operators at Mission Control covered their ears and backed away from the speakers.

This time Buzz Aldrin stopped, as if frozen in space.

'It's working!' said Walter. '3-2-1: **ZZUB**

NIRDLA, ZZUB NIRDLA, ZZUB NIRDLA!'

Slowly, Buzz began to move back towards the lunar module on the same trajectory on which he had floated away.

The Ruby Giftstone faded once more.

'Foiled again,' said Grandad. 'There's something preventing the portal from making contact. Let's take a little break.'

'Mint, anybody?' said Annie sarcastically.

'Very funny,' said Levon.

With that, the Ruby Giftstone glowed so brightly they all had to cover their eyes.

'What's happening?' said Peggy.

'That stone is on fire,' said Harry.

Levon and Annie looked at each other in alarm. They knew what it meant.

'Walter has used his last gift,' said Grandad.

'What do you mean?' said Harry.

'If we fail to bring him home . . . he . . .'

'What are you saying?' said Peggy.

'He'll be stuck in the past for ever! MINTS!!!'

A Gib Pets Rof A Llams Nam

Buzz Aldrin landed at the module's entrance and was hauled inside by Neil Armstrong and Walter.

'Can you believe it?' said Buzz. 'We get to the moon without a hitch and then the darn ladder breaks. Thanks, Walter. I knew you'd bring me back.'

'I couldn't have done it without the Commander's help,' said Walter.

'I was very much second in command,' said Neil.

'Did nobody think of testing the ladder?' asked Buzz.

Neil Armstrong shook his head. 'They reckoned a ladder is a ladder. What could go wrong?'

Buzz Aldrin turned to Neil Armstrong. 'Commander, something tells me I'm not meant to be the first man to walk on the moon.'

'Funny you should say that,' said Neil Armstrong. 'Something tells me I'm not either!'

'But somebody has to do it!' said Walter.

'Exactly!' said Neil Armstrong. 'You should have the honour, Vice Commander.'

'I second that!' said Buzz Aldrin.

'B-b-but . . .' stuttered Walter, 'Mission Control has ordered me to stay inside the lunar landing module!'

'As Flight Commander of the crew of Apollo 11, I hereby order you to be the first man to walk on the surface of the moon,' said Neil Armstrong. 'Here's the plan: Buzz will film your descent to the moon from right here, while I will say, "This is one big step for Man, one giant leap for mankind" . . .'

'One big step for "a" man,' said Walter.

'Oh yeah,' said Neil Armstrong before continuing, 'then I will descend the ladder and you and I will swap places, while Buzz moves the camera away from you to film the moon surface. At no time will any more than one astronaut be visible. Nobody will know except us. Any questions?'

'No, Commander,' said Buzz Aldrin.

'No . . . Commander . . . Armstrong,' said Walter, fear and excitement igniting in his head.

Walter placed his right foot on the top step of the ladder.

Back in Grandad's room, Grandad, Peggy, Harry, Levon and Annie were now holding hands and forming a circle around Grandad, who was sitting, propped upright by his pillows. The wheelbarrow was empty and the mint wrappers in the centre of the floor almost reached to the ceiling.

'Walter Speazlebud! Walter Speazlebud! Walter Speazlebud!' they chanted, eyes closed, brows scrunched in concentration. Louder and louder they chanted, until the flower-patterned lampshade above their heads began to vibrate as if being shaken by an earthquake.

Even from behind the lids of their closed

eyes, they could see the orange glow of the Ruby Giftstone. It made them feel as if they were on a beach in the midday sun.

'I think we can do it this time!' said Grandad. 'We can bring him home this time!'

One careful step at a time, Walter climbed down the broken ladder until he reached the last step, just millimetres from the moon's surface. He stopped dead. There was a circle of **Noitanigami** just centimetres from his navel, but this one was unlike the others – this one was as thick as cigar smoke.

'No, Grandad, not now, NOT NOW!'

'Go for it, Neil,' shouted Dr Gordon, as he and his comrades at Mission Control rose to their feet and cheered him on.

'Walter Speazlebud! Walter Speazlebud! Walter Speazlebud!' they all shouted at the top of their voices. The Ruby Giftstone was now glowing like lava pouring from the mouth of a volcano.

'Once more,' shouted Grandad. 'We have him this time. Let's take my grandson home!'

'Walter Speazlebud, Walter Speazlebud, Walter Speaz–'

Nurse Hartnett burst into the room with such ferocity that the door hinges pinged against the wall, and the door fell with a dull thud on to the mound of mint wrapping papers.

In shock, everyone opened their eyes, stopped chanting and stared at the furious nurse.

'Shaaaadup!' she yelled.

The Ruby Giftstone lost its glow like a firefly in a rainstorm.

'I followed the trail of mints, then I heard the shouting,' said the nurse furiously. 'Have you no regard for the rules of this institution. And what's this?'

'A wheelbarrow,' said Grandad timidly.

'The gardener's wheelbarrow! I have a right to call the police.'

'We're trying to bring Walter home. He's . . . lost in space,' explained Grandad.

'He's stuck back in 1969,' said Peggy, wiping her tears away.

'So are you,' snapped Nurse Hartnett, 'if those clothes you're wearing are anything to go by.'

'He's gone to the moon,' said Annie.

'He's the Vice Commander of the Apollo 11 mission,' said Levon.

'I'm staring at a bunch of lunatics,' said Nurse Hartnett. 'Is nobody aware that Arnold Speazlebud is a sick man? I want anybody who is not family to leave *now*. Visiting hours are over.'

Walter closed his eyes. He was sure he was about to be sucked into the mist portal and spat out at the top of Nittiburg Hill. He opened them again slowly, one at a time. He was still standing on the last rung of the lunar ladder, and the portal had disappeared! He placed his left foot on the surface of the moon.

'That's one big step for a small man,' he said silently, with a huge smile.

'That's one small step for Man, one giant leap for mankind,' said Neil Armstrong through his microphone, from inside the lunar module.

'He said it again!' said Walter, shaking his head. 'It should be one step for *a* man!'

The moon's surface was soft and crunchy beneath Walter's feet. He looked up to see the earth, a marbled, blue-and-white globe floating in a pool of stars, and, for the first time since the mission began he felt no fear, no fear at all, only a peaceful feeling tinged with joy.

He bounced about in zero gravity, as if on a trampoline, leaving deep footprints as he landed, then catapulting himself into space once again. With a smile as big as the sun, he bent down and picked up a small rock. He threw it, and watched it float into space. Then he picked up some more for the people in his life he wished were with him right now.

All too soon, Neil Armstrong appeared at the hatch. It was time to swap places.

How the earth appeared to Walter as he
stood on the moon.

The famous photograph of Neil Armstrong taken
by Buzz Aldrin. But doesn't he look a bit small?
Could this be a photograph taken of Walter
Speazlebud – and are there many others that
NASA do not want us to see?

Walter climbed up the ladder and back into the lunar module. Through the window he could see Neil Armstrong plant the American flag in the moon-sand and Buzz lay a plaque, which read:

Here Men from Planet Earth
First Set Foot Upon the Moon.
July AD 1969
We Came in Peace for all Mankind.

Men and a boy, thought Walter proudly.

As soon as Annie and Levon had left the room, Nurse Hartnett instructed Grandad to lie back on his pillows and rest.

'We've got to keep trying!' pleaded Peggy. 'We have to bring my Walter back.'

'Leave Arnold alone,' said Nurse Hartnett. 'All that shouting and roaring has worn him out.' Then she took a bottle of smelling salts from her pocket and wafted it under his nostrils.

'How will we get Walter back now?' cried Peggy.

'He'll be fine,' said Harry, putting his arm around his wife. 'I know he's going to be fine.'

Yrrah Steg Hcir

Bob Speazlebud and Wynter Blossombloom were sitting in a café on the Florida coast when a newsflash came on the radio.

'Early this morning, eight days, three hours, eighteen minutes and eighteen seconds after leaving the Kennedy Space Center, the crew of Apollo 11 parachuted into the Pacific Ocean 380 kilometres south of Johnston Island. They have arrived home safely.'

'Yeeeeaaah!' shouted Bob, jumping to his feet. 'You made it, Walter! Time to get back to work.'

Later that day, Walter sat in the front seat of the limousine, holding a pair of lunar boots in his lap.

'I see you kept your boots as souvenirs,' said Bob.

'These boots belong to Commander Armstrong. He wanted mine!'

'You must have played a very important part in the mission.'

Walter smiled.

'Did you walk on the moon?' Bob asked.

'Maybe,' said Walter with a wink.

Bob winked back. 'Your secret is safe with me. How much time do you have left?'

Walter looked at his watch. 'About half an hour if it all goes to plan. Grandad said he'd bring me back at eight o'clock.'

Later, Bob sat on the front lawn while Walter performed various stretches.

'Yoga?' said Bob.

'Pre-time-travel stretch routine,' said Walter.

'I'll miss you, kid,' said Bob. 'You've been an inspiration. You followed your dreams and changed the course of history.'

'I'll miss you, too, Bob,' said Walter. 'I'll miss 1969.' He finished his stretches, reached into his travel bag and took out a small rock. 'Genuine moon rock,' he said as he handed it to Bob. 'I picked it myself.'

A car pulled up outside the gate. The passenger door opened and a small bald man in a black suit hopped out. 'Vice Commander Speazlebud?' he called out.

'That's me,' said Walter, walking over to the gate.

'I am so glad to have intercepted you before you leave,' the man said, shaking Walter's hand vigorously. 'My name is Zlander Ovsky.'

'The moon-buggy designer!' said Walter.

'We have decided to go for it,' Zlander said.

'Go for what?' said Walter.

'The Speazlebud Synchronised Suspension System, of course. We want to incorporate it into our space-buggy design.' He handed Walter an envelope. 'There's a cheque enclosed, which I hope will be acceptable to your father. We have increased our normal fee by five thousand per cent to allow for inflation in the future. NASA will have the rights to use the Speazlebud Synchronised Suspension System for thirty years, which means that, when your father invents the system in the new century, he will own it fully.'

'If it's not acceptable I'll come back and let you know,' said Walter, smiling.

Zlander Ovsky saluted, and returned to his car.

'I think my dad has just become rich,' said Walter with a beaming smile as he sat down on the grass beside Bob, who was still staring at his moon rock. But as Walter checked his watch once more, the smile disappeared from his face. 'I'm still here! It's been nearly an hour! I hope Grandad's OK!'

Back in room number seventeen, Grandad was quietly singing 'Danny Boy' backwards, while Nurse Hartnett took his temperature with a deeply puzzled expression. 'His temperature is normal,' said Nurse Hartnett, 'but, judging by his singing, he's not well at all. I should call Doctor Donaghy.'

'He's been singing that song backwards all his life,' said Harry. 'This is a good sign!'

Peggy just stared at the ground blankly. 'My boy,' she repeated over and over.

Just then, a newsflash came on the TV: 'NASA have just announced that the Astralgazer Superzoom is now fully operational. The world's most powerful telescope has located the American flag, and the footprints left behind by the Apollo astronauts.'

Grandad stopped singing. 'Turn it up,' he said, sitting bolt upright without Nurse Hartnett's help.

'There have been many conspiracy theories suggesting that the moon landing was faked. Today those theories were dismissed for good as the Astralgazer telescope provided conclusive evidence that Man had walked on the surface of the moon. However, a new mystery has come to light. It seems that there are not two but *three* sets of footsteps on the moon. Who was the third astronaut? And how many years will it take to solve *that* one? I'm Trebor Gartons for ABD News.'

'He did it!' shouted Grandad. 'Walter walked on the moon!'

'You're raving,' said Nurse Hartnett. 'Doctor!'

'I want my son back!' said Peggy.

Grandad looked at the clock. 'He's probably back at Bob's place in Florida by now,' he said, his voice clear and crisp. 'Time to bring him home.'

'Should we get you some more mints?' said Peggy, new hope lighting up her face.

'I don't need any mints!' said Grandad. 'My grandson has just walked on the moon. Walter Speazlebud! Walter Speazlebud! Walter Speazle-bud!' he chanted.

'Don't start this again,' said Nurse Hartnett, looking up to heaven.

Grandad stopped. 'That should do the trick,' he said to Peggy. 'Walter should be home any minute now. MISSION ACCOMPLISHED!'

'What's that?' said Bob.

A fully formed mist portal was drifting towards Walter on the evening breeze. It was the best yet – a premier-division, first-in-the-class, gold-medal portal.

'The old codger is alive and kicking,' said Bob, giving Walter a high five.

'Bye bye, Bob . . .' called Walter, as the portal made contact and he disappeared.

'Goodbye, Walter,' whispered Bob, as the portal hung momentarily in the air before fading away. 'See you in the future. I hope I'm not too grumpy when we meet again!'

Eht Oreh Snruter

Walter sat on a bench looking around him. He wasn't on Nittiburg Hill, he was . . . at the end of Bob and Gertrude's garden! Further up the garden a man stood with his back to Walter, weeding a vegetable patch.

'Bob?' Walter called out.

The man turned around. He looked like Granduncle Bob . . . but much trimmer and healthier, and he didn't walk with a stoop!

'Is it really you, Bob?'

'Yes, time-traveller, it's me,' he said, taking the piece of moon rock that Walter had given him from his pocket. 'Thanks again, Walter. I'll treasure this for ever.'

Now that he was closer, Walter could see that the lines on Bob's brow were much softer than before, and his hair, which had been almost white, had only hints of grey. He seemed happier too, like somebody had switched a light on inside him and burned away the darkness.

'After you left, NASA asked me to come back – as their Chief Engineer,' said Bob. 'I worked there for twenty more years before I retired. I've had a wonderful life.'

Bob turned and gestured for Walter to follow him. 'Come on, kiddo, now you've got to meet my *new*, wonderful wife.'

Oh no! thought Walter. *Wynter Blossombloom has replaced Aunt Gertrude!*

'I'm gonna wash my hands,' said Bob as they entered the kitchen. 'You go ahead into the sitting room.'

With a heavy heart, Walter walked down the corridor and stopped outside the sitting room door. He opened it slowly, and then his heart missed a beat. There, standing at the window, watering a plant with her back turned, was a woman with *blonde* hair. He coughed.

The woman turned her head slightly to the side.

'Hello,' he said.

She turned around. 'Welcome back, Walter, and well done! Bob's been telling me everything!!'

'Aunt Gertrude! You look twenty years younger!'

'Isn't she a stunner?' said Bob, appearing behind him. '*My* Wynter Blossombloom.'

'No . . .' said Walter, confused. 'She's Gertrude.'

'I was Wynter Blossombloom,' said Gertrude, 'but it's a silly name. When Bob and I got married I decided to use my middle name, Gertrude, instead. Still need proof?' she said, her eyes twinkling as she rolled up her sleeve. 'Here's my tattoo.'

Walter breathed a sigh of relief.

'Now let's phone your parents,' said Bob. 'You've had a long day. I'm sure you want to go home!'

Eht Hturt Ta Tsal

The following morning Walter sat by Grandad's bedside as tiny snores escaped from his mouth. 'Grandad, it's me.'

Grandad Speazlebud opened his eyes. 'Walter,' he said, reaching out his hand. 'You've come back safely.'

'I discovered the truth,' said Walter, placing a piece of moon stone in Grandad's hand.

'And you made what was meant to be, be,' said Grandad proudly.

Walter spoke in a whisper. '*I saw eht tsrif nam ot klaw no eht noom*!'

'*Uoy ees*, *Retlaw*,' said Grandad, '*Gnihtyna si elbissop*.'

'I already thought that, Grandad. Now I believe it.'

'I couldn't have said it better myself,' replied Grandad, as Walter helped him to sit up. Grandad reached over, took the Ruby Giftstone from its box and put the moon stone in its place. He placed the Giftstone in Walter's outstretched hand, asked him to close it, then he cupped both his hands around Walter's. 'In the name of **Noitanigami**, I deem you, Walter Anthony Speazlebud, worthy to be called Keeper of the Ruby Giftstone. You have earned this title by using your gifts with bravery and honour. Guided by *The Book of Noitanigami*, I ask you to use your gifts wisely.'

Walter felt like the Giftstone was glowing right in the centre of his heart. 'Thanks for accidentally sending Annie on the adventure, too!' he said.

'In the world of **Noitanigami** there are no such things as accidents,' said Grandad with a wink. 'Only happy coincidences.'

'So, it was no accident that I landed in Bob's garden instead of Nittiburg Hill.'

'Oh,' said Grandad, 'now that *was* an accident. I hope he wasn't too annoyed?'

'Annoyed?' said Bob, standing at the place

where the door used to be, immaculately dressed in a grey suit with a red handkerchief sticking out of the breast pocket.

The expression on Grandad's face was the same expression Walter imagined he himself had worn at the moment Neil Armstrong asked him to come to the moon. Grandad opened his arms wide. 'My brother has come back to me!'

Walter slipped out of the room as the two brothers embraced for the first time in over three decades.

In the hallway Doctor Donaghy was in deep conversation with Harry and Peggy. 'Ah, Walter,' said Harry, as the doctor walked away, 'we need to talk to you for a moment.'

Harry, Peggy and Walter sat together in the waiting room at the end of the hallway. 'Grandad is coming home,' said Harry.

'But Mum said you couldn't look after him any more,' said Walter.

'He will have daytime help,' said Peggy, taking Walter's hand in hers. 'Nurse Hartnett will be his full-time carer. She's actually very fond of him.'

'I know,' said Walter.

'The cheque that I received from NASA will cover all the expenses,' said Harry, 'and allow us to convert the garage into a bedroom so that Grandad doesn't have to go up those stairs any more.' There was a look in Harry's eyes that said he had something else to say, something difficult.

'Walter,' said Harry gently, 'Doctor Donaghy has just told us . . . Grandad does not have very long to live. He believes that he has been hanging on for this moment – to be re-united with his brother again – and now he can let go.'

Walter nodded understandingly. After all, Grandad had been preparing him for this for a long time now. But they didn't know that Walter had a plan, a wonderful plan that would put a smile right back on everybody's faces.

Later that evening, Walter pushed Grandad in his wheelchair down Nittiburg Hill to the carved wooden bench overlooking the village. 'You know, Grandad, I don't think I've returned to normal yet,' said Walter. 'When I look at the village down there, I see a bunch of buildings hitching a ride on the back of a planet as it floats in space while it circles the sun.'

'And when I look at nature,' said Grandad, 'I see grass that's alive and breathing and tingling with an electric lushness, and trees that look like sleeping giants, their branches like fingers reaching out to touch the sky. It's called being *alive*.'

'Grandad,' said Walter, excitedly, 'there's something I want to say. Now that I'm keeper of the Ruby Giftstone, I can reverse you so that you become younger again, and even more *alive* than you are now, and we can go fishing together and you won't have to be old and –'

'Stop,' said Grandad gently but firmly. 'My dear Walter, I have been on this planet for over eighty years, and I have lived every day as if it were my last. Yes, I am coming to the end of my days. It may be tomorrow, it may be next week, it may be next year, but when my time is up, my time is up. And when it comes I will throw my arms around that moment like I throw my arms around this moment I am spending, right now, with you.'

Walter felt a dart of hurt pierce his heart. 'But, Grandad . . . wouldn't you like to stay here, so that we can spend more time together?'

'Walter, I will not ask God for one second more than he wishes to give me in this life. Do you see that setting sun? Should we call it back and ask the moon to wait?'

Walter thought about it for a moment. 'I suppose not,' he replied, and then grinned. 'I love the moon! I couldn't ask it to wait!'

Lla Steb Era Ffo

'You really walked on the moon . . . *first*?' said Levon, as he and Walter walked to school through the village on Tuesday morning. 'No wonder you were too tired to see me or Annie yesterday.'

'I was pooped,' replied Walter, 'and I spent all evening with Grandad. You know, I *almost* didn't walk on the moon at all. You were all trying to bring me home!'

'I wasn't trying too hard,' said Levon. 'I didn't want to ruin your adventure.'

Walter gave his best friend a high five.

'And I don't think Annie was either,' said Levon.

'I have something for you,' said Walter. He stopped, reached into his bag and took out his telescope. 'It's yours, Levon. You were head of Mission Control. You did a great job. You even ate Mrs Frost's Xtra Strong Mints for me!'

'No,' said Levon, 'you won the bet. You won a kitten.'

'You earned a telescope.'

'I can't take your telescope,' said Levon. 'It's not fair. How will you watch the moon at night?'

'Bob is giving me his. It's super-duper. When I'm older I'm going to take it into the city at night so that people can see the moon up close.'

Levon pointed the telescope in the direction of the school. 'Well, I may not be an astronomer, but I reckon I have spotted a particular star called Annus Zuckerius shooting into school before us. We must be *really* late.'

'Maybe she's turned over a new leaf!'

'I bet you'll marry her some day,' said Levon. 'I bet my black rabbit.'

'No more silly bets . . .' said Walter, a hint of red tinting his cheeks.

'You're right,' said Levon. 'For every bet there's a fool and thief. I was a fool yesterday evening.'

'You were?'

'I lost two guinea pigs, three books, a slice of mouldy cheese and a Gameboy.'

'Maybe this will make up for it,' said Walter, taking a piece of moon rock from his pocket and placing it in his hand.

'Moon rock as well!!!'

'You can sell it and buy all the guinea pigs, books, cheese and Gameboys you want!'

Spetstoof No Eht Noom

'Who's missing?' said Miss O'Connor, peering over the rim of her reading glasses.

'Spittlesuds and Hoppedy,' said Gary Crannick.

'Mr Crannick, I see that you've turned over a new leaf,' said Miss O'Connor, sarcastically.

The door opened and Walter and Levon walked in.

'Take your seats, boys, and please be on time tomorrow.'

Nobody said anything but, as Walter strolled towards his seat, in his trainers, worn jeans and faded 60's T-shirt, words appeared in people's minds. 'Confident' was the word that occurred to Miss O'Connor. Annie thought of the word 'glowing', as Walter sat down directly in front of her. Even Gary Crannick grimaced, as he fought desperately to suppress the word 'respect'.

'OK,' said Miss O'Connor, clapping her hands to command everybody's attention. 'We've all seen it on TV and read about it in the Sunday papers. The Astralgazer Superzoom, which is now up and running, has discovered not two, but *three* pairs of footsteps on the moon. Any guesses as to who the third astronaut might be?'

'I bet it was an alien following the astronauts,' said Nadia Eflow.

'I still think it was all filmed in a studio,' said Eva Hearne. 'My mum says not to believe anything you hear on the news.'

As a debate developed, Annie, Walter and Levon sat quietly with their arms folded and contented smiles on their faces. Walter tapped Annie's toe with the heel of his shoe, then reached his hand behind his back and dropped a piece of moon stone on to her desk.

She took it in her hands and closed her eyes.

Levon leaned over and whispered in her ear, 'Isn't that the best present anybody has ever given you in your life? He gave me one, too.'

This close-up from the Astralgazer Superzoom telescope clearly shows Neil Armstrong's footprint alongside one of Walter's. Is it any wonder that scientists continue to be baffled by this discovery?

'It's nice,' she whispered back, 'but it's not as nice as having you two as friends.' Then she leaned forward and whispered to Walter, 'You and me, we're going diving after school, Moon Man.'

Eugolipe

Walter lay in his bed, Neil Armstrong's moon boots dangling from a peg on the wall above his head. He had watched the full moon creep into the window frame until it sat dead centre. It looked like a picture hanging on the wall of heaven. He sat up, reached over and brought the powerful new telescope that Bob had given him to his left eye. Then he adjusted the focus until the moon was so close he was sure he could see his own footprints in the sand.

He heard his grandad singing next door and it made him smile.

> *'Ho Ynnad Yob,*
> *Eht sepip eht sepip era gnillac,*
> *Morf nelg ot nelg*
> *Dna nwod eht niatnuom edis . . .'*

He knew that Grandad, too, could see that big old moon through his window, lighting up the sky, calling men and women to venture in the heavens. Walter took a deep breath and joined in.

> *'Eht s'remmus enog*
> *dna lla eht sevael era gniyd*
> *sit uoy sit uoy*
> *tsum og dna I tsum edib* . . .'

They sang together, the moon illuminating their faces, until Grandad's voice gradually became quieter, then faded like the stars at dawn.

Stnemegdelwonkca

Many, many thanks to the following: Eve Golden-Woods, Aidan Ravitch, Kirsten Sheridan, Frank Golden, Berry Guthrie, Eoin Murphy, Aoife and Bronagh Jordan, Conall McGrath, Hugh Keenan, Ronan Keenan, Alison O'Neill, Eugene McNeill, Amelia Caulfield, Berne Kiely, Trish McAdam, Mark Kilroy, the students and teachers of the Bishop Foley Primary School, Carlow, Michelle Nolan, Lisa Wolfe, Geraldine Bigelow, Julie Lemberger, Douglas Gresham, Brendan Harding, Bernard and Angela Jennings, Alison and Eva Hearne, Geraldine Byrne, Denis Lonergan, Maurice Whitmore, Nicola Greene, Lara Agnew, Michael Gavshon, Barney Cordell, Katryn Kinser, Clare Naylor, Sheila Carroll, Kenny Gronningsater, Eoin Colfer, Grace Wells, my agent Sophie Hicks, Sheila Prattke and all the staff of the Tyrone Guthrie Centre in

Annaghmakerrig, my editor Cally Poplak and all the wonderful folk at Egmont.

Nehw uoy evah detanimile eht elbissopmi, revetahw sniamer, revewoh elbaborpmi, tsum eb eht hturt

Ris Ruhtra Nanoc Elyod